The Legend of the S

MyGreyhound Publishing

This book contains a greyhound sighting.
adele@mygreypub.com

For my son, Joshua

Table of Contents

Chapter One

As Camelia Wright turned the bend, three miles out from the Lost and Found Antique Shop in Devon, England, she realized that, in her haste to close early, she had forgotten to take the vintage Caravelle wristwatch she had promised to bring to Mrs. Walker. Knowing that turning back now would further delay her arrival at her sister's birthday party, she hesitated. Darn the luck, *Camelia thought.* Mrs. Walker was so looking forward to receiving that watch. *Her mind made up, she turned around and headed back to the shop.*

The late afternoon sun still offered enough illumination to fill the shop, as Camelia went straight to the back office to retrieve the forgotten watch. There it is, just where I left it, *she thought, reaching out to take the watch from the desktop. Turning to leave, Camelia suddenly froze. As she drew in a strong gasp, her eyes fixed on the body of a young woman lying motionless on the floor.*

Then, a sound, a sound of someone in the shop. Her mind was racing—who is this woman—is she dead—perhaps he didn't see me; *and then, she heard the footsteps coming closer ....*

It had been so quiet in the cramped bedroom/converted office that he jumped when the phone rang.

"David speaking," he said instinctively, as his concentration was suddenly interrupted from his writing.

"Good afternoon, David, I heard you were in town. This is Ellen from Stuart Cove Realty. Do you remember me?"

"Yes, of course, I do. I think the last time I saw you, you had come by to join us for a picnic, but instead, there

1

was a horrible rainstorm."

"I was soaked to the bone in the time it took me to get from my car to the front door. We ended up having the picnic on the porch, if I recall correctly," Ellen said.

"Yes, I was very disappointed because I was supposed to meet some friends at the park. I remember it distinctly. Isn't it funny—those things we remember?"

"David, I'm so sorry to hear about your Aunt Gina's passing. She was a fine lady and a very close friend of mine."

"Thank you, I know she was up in years, but I had imagined her outliving us all. She was a woman content with life, even during hard times."

"Yes, if we all could be as fortunate," Ellen responded. "At first, I was worried about her after she lost Walter, but she seemed to hold up—I guess because she spent so much of their married life on her own while he was out at sea."

"You're right," David responded. "She was a strong woman, but I think it became difficult those last few years. I know it was hard on her when my mom passed away. They were very close."

"True, after your mom passed, you were all she had left," Ellen paused. "We'll miss her terribly." Changing the conversation's tone, Ellen said, "She always spoke so highly of you. She admired your courage going off to live in New York to work for a big newspaper business."

"Well, I don't know how much courage it took, really."

"For a lady who never left her hometown, she was very impressed with your ambition."

"If I had grown up here, I might never have left. But growing up in Philly—well, New York doesn't seem like that big a jump."

"She was very proud of you. I hope you know that."

"Thank you, it means a lot to me."

"So, do you have a girlfriend?" Ellen asked.

David, a good-looking man of twenty-six, was of medium build. He sported a businessman's haircut but wore it slightly longer than most men in his circle of friends and co-workers did. He would often run his hand through his long bangs to keep them out of his eyes. Most notable was his smile. It was not just his straight white teeth, but also the glimmer in his dark brown eyes, that made most people smile back without realizing it. He tried to stay in shape by going to the local gym a few days a week, which had the added benefit of relieving some stress he had because of his job. David was ambitious, both in college and early in his career. His professional goals included attaining an executive position in a leading media company. He believed he could meet his objective in New York, and he lived his life toward that end. Unfortunately, his goals left little time for any type of serious relationship, something that became clear when, nearly a year ago, he found himself involved with a young woman who abruptly ended the relationship because she believed he was spending too much time at work, and not with her.

"No, not at this time," David answered, a little embarrassed by the question.

"Well, I almost forgot the reason for my call. I hope you don't mind if I turn the conversation to business, but I wanted to offer my services in case you're interested in selling the property, assuming that is what you would like to do. Of course, if you choose to use it as a rental property, I can help with that as well. People are very interested in moving to this area. Have you decided what you would like to do with the place?"

"Yes," David answered, "I have thought about it and have decided to go ahead and sell it. I was able to arrange a short absence from work, and I have a friend currently staying at my place while he looks for an apartment in the city. That gives me a little time to get the house ready to sell, and I'll use any extra time to finish writing my novel."

"A novel—how exciting. I think that is a great idea. It is very quiet there at the cottage. I'm sure it would be perfect for writing."

The cottage, while only a short drive from town, was an especially tranquil place to write. With few neighbors on the dead-end road, the property included about half an acre of land on Kings Creek. A small pier, a popular spot for the local ducks and seagulls, reached out from the backyard. The home itself was a modest one-and-a-half-story bungalow with two bedrooms, a galley-style kitchen, and a small cozy living room. Off the living room, next to the fireplace, a door led to a screened porch. In the warmth of the Connecticut summers, this room got the most use. You could look out to the water from here and usually rely on a cool breeze. A worn auburn couch sat against the wall, and a long wooden table with a red-and-white checkered tablecloth was positioned in the middle of the room with a mismatch of chairs around it. On each end facing the creek were rocking chairs, the cushions tattered from many years of use. There was plenty of room for family and friends to get together for a feast of clams or a quiet evening sipping iced tea.

"I could meet with you on Friday. I'll come by the house, say around ten in the morning. Would that be good for you?"

"Yes, that would be fine. I'm glad you called. It'll be nice seeing you again."

"I better let you go, David. It sounds as if you have a lot of work to do."

"See you Friday, Ellen."

After hanging up the phone, David turned back to his laptop.

... She quickly hid behind the desk, hoping he would not hear her fear....

David paused, sat back, and listened. The window was open, and a warm June breeze blew the white lace curtains into the room. He could hear the angry calls of the gulls fighting for a place on the pier pilings.

I'm supposed to be getting this place ready to sell, so I shouldn't feel guilty if I take a break.

As he walked from room to room, surveying the work needing to be done, David began to wonder what life must have been like for his aunt as a fisherman's wife. He stepped into the master bedroom and noticed a framed picture sitting on the dresser. Although it had always been there, it now attracted his attention. Looking at the black-and-white photograph, David saw his aunt and uncle in their wedding attire looking back at him. They were very young. Could they have known then, the life they would live together? David knew the answer because that life was the life of nearly all the families in Stuart Cove back then. They lived a hard, simple life. They did not have much, but they had what they needed. David's own mother decided she wanted something different, so she went off to college in Philadelphia where she met his father.

Looking closely at the faces, he admired their devotion to each other, not only apparent in the photograph, but also each time he had seen them together throughout the years he visited. The times David spent with his uncle were especially memorable. His earliest recollection was at age nine. It was summer, and David and his grandparents, his parents, and Uncle Walter were all there to celebrate Aunt Gina's sixty-seventh birthday. It was a warm day, and Granddad and Grandma each sat back in the rocking chairs, looking out to the pier from the screened porch. They kept David's dad in conversation about the local gossip and weather, as the women were busy in the kitchen getting lunch together.

Lying on the floor, looking at his *Cat in the Hat* book, David noticed his uncle motioning to follow him down to the pier. David jumped up and ran to join him. It was there that he observed his uncle in his element, pointing out the egret walking on the shoreline and a kingfisher perched on a nearby tree branch. He was a large man with strong arms, dark skin, and a ruddy complexion—very different from the men in his own hometown. The real treat came when David's uncle would reach into his pocket and pull out a rope.

"Do you want me to show you a knot?"

"Of course, I do," said the young boy with a grin from ear to ear.

"What knot would you like me to show you?"

"A bowline," David replied.

He would watch intently, as his uncle with his large calloused hands would perform his magic. With the knot complete, he would hold it up for the young boy to inspect.

"Now, you do it."

With his uncle's kind guidance, David would slowly turn and loop the rope until he, too, could hold up his achievement for examination.

Seventeen years later, and the voices filling the house then were now absent. A sense of sadness came over David.

Well, I guess it's a good time to take a trip into town, he thought, gently placing the picture back on the dresser. David went downstairs, walked across the living room, and paused at the door to the porch, from where he could see the pier. After a moment, he turned back and left through the front door.

It was evening by this time, as David pulled out of the driveway and onto the gravel road. *I wonder how long it will take to sell this house,* he thought, driving toward town. He reflected on his conversation with Ellen and her mentioning that tourists, otherwise known as outsiders by the locals, were really showing an interest in the area. David turned onto the main road, this time fully aware of his surroundings. It was a pleasant evening with the sun beginning its slow descent and the tall maple and oak trees casting their shadows on the road. With the windows down, David could smell the summer, as it brought back peaceful memories of his past visits. *Why does this area appear greener this time,* he pondered, driving along the quiet road.

It was not long before David approached town. He made a left turn onto Main Street, placing him at a slight decline, looking down from which he could see the small harbor of Stuart Cove. As he drove through town, David entered an area barely touched by time. Neighboring families had run many businesses lining the street for generations, including J&J's Shoe Store; Wilson's, a small department store; Joe's Family Restaurant; and Ricky's Grocery Store. Even the bank manager began his career at the bank as a young man, just as his father did before him. David noticed a few new shops in town, though: a crafts store, an antique shop, and a bakery. Physically, downtown consisted of several other streets where you could find the courthouse or the county library. It was Main Street that attracted the activity: young boys chasing each other and ducking into the shop doorways when possible, people taking care of their shopping and socializing at every opportunity, tourists taking in the nostalgia. Closer to the harbor was Johnson's Hardware, where many local men would congregate if they were not at the Fishhook Pub located almost next door at the bottom of Main Street.

A cold brewsky would hit the spot right now, David thought, pulling into the parking area outside the pub. Stepping out of his car, he took in the sights—the fishing boats with all their rigging, the many seagulls flying overhead and resting on the pilings. He even noticed a tan-colored cat strolling toward the dock house. David decided to take a detour and walk down to the docks for a moment; the seagulls showed their displeasure by screaming and flying off, as he approached. Reaching the end of the pier, he looked out past the many sailboats anchored in the cove and saw the Stone Ridge Lighthouse. The bright white tower sat out on the Point some distance from the cove. Something about that lighthouse—it always fascinated him, but David never really knew why. He decided that it probably affected everyone that way, and without another thought about it, he turned back. As he passed the fishing boats, he read the names carefully painted on the sterns—*The Ruth*, *Prowler*, *Shane*, *Seagull*, *Shirley Anne II*, and *Jetty*. These names contrasted starkly to the yachts of New York David would sometimes see. They instead would display such names as *Dad's Toy*, *Deeper in Debt*, or *Spare Time*. He chuckled, as he headed for the pub, thinking about the disparity.

Approaching the pub, David felt his cell phone vibrate in his pocket. Checking the display, he noticed it was Russ from work.

"Hey, Russ, what's up?" David answered, slightly irritated to receive a call from work.

"David, I can't find your file regarding

Congressman Attwood, and I have to get that story out."

"I put all my active files out on the D drive, so they could be accessed by anyone who needs them. Did you look there?"

"I thought I did," Russ said, as he checked.

"There it is. Sorry, David, I just started to panic."

"You're on your own while I'm here. I told you I don't have Internet access. Besides, I have a lot to take care of here, so my mind's on other things; that's why I took time off. Now, will you be okay?"

"Yea, I'll try not to call you—my mistake," Russ apologized.

David felt bad about how he had spoken to Russ, but he knew if he were not firm with his co-worker, Russ would take the easy route and continue to call any time something came up, rather than handle it himself.

As he entered the pub, it took David a moment to acclimate to the darker surroundings. In front of him was the bar, jutting out into an open area. Along the walls were booths, and in the rear were a couple of pool tables. The afternoon sun did not reach the small multi-pane windows looking out to the harbor. To David's right was a young couple sitting at a booth. They were in deep conversation, not even stopping to notice that someone new had entered. Several people sat at the bar, and most paused to look in his direction—just for a moment, though, before they returned to their conversations. David approached the bar and sat down.

"What can I get you this evening?" the bartender asked in a scruffy but friendly tone.

"What do you have on tap?"

"We have Sam Adams, Michelob, and Harpoon."

"I'll take a Sam Adams, please."

"Coming right up," she said and turned to grab a glass.

Now that his eyes had adjusted, he could observe the pub's patrons. There was a middle-aged couple sitting across from him. They were both smoking cigarettes, one nodding as the other spoke. He had the feeling they had been there for some time and would be there for some time to come.

"Here ya go."

"Thanks."

David took a long drink and placed the glass down on the bar before returning to his inspection. Sitting to the couple's right were two young men who seemed to be having a friendly argument about where tomorrow's best fishing would be. He was not trying to listen to their conversation, but they were speaking a bit loud, considering no one else was competing to be heard.

David took another drink, and as he lowered the glass, he noticed an old man sitting at the far end of the bar. *Now doesn't this guy match the classic waterman*, David thought, attempting to take the guy in without being obvious. The old man appeared to have a full head of white hair under his black Greek fisherman's cap. His dark tan stood out in contrast to his white beard. The deep lines in his face told of the many years he had spent on the water. As he sat there nursing a beer, no one seemed to be aware of him, nor did he seem aware of others, giving David an anomalous feeling. He was not sure if he should feel sorry for the guy or a little worried.

David then noticed he was not the only one inspecting someone; the bartender seemed to take a new interest in him.

"Are you Gina's nephew?" she asked.

"Yes, David Parker," he said, standing and reaching his hand out to her.

"Mary Carson," she said, taking his hand and giving it a firm shake. Mary, a woman in her middle forties and a native of the town, owned the Fishhook Pub. She was extremely well liked by the locals, especially the menfolk. They felt comfortable with her, as if she were one of the guys. Mary took care of them when they stopped by. She had a way about her that kept them in line, and they respected that. She was a large, but solid, woman. She had especially strong arms, never allowing anyone to help her with the heavy lifting. Her male co-workers and patrons no longer attempted to help, because they knew she would snap at them for trying.

"Well, I'll be damned," she said, "I thought that was you."

She paused. "Sure was sorry to hear of her passing."

"Yes, I'm going to miss her."

"Do you guys think you could keep it down a bit? Can't you see I'm trying to have a conversation!" Mary yelled at the two men whose argument was getting louder.

"But Jim here is nuts. He doesn't know what he's talking about," one man yelled back at Mary.

"Neither one of you know what the hell you're talking about, so keep it down!"

They turned back to their argument, but this time at a slightly lower volume.

"So, are you going to be moving here?" Mary asked, as she turned her interest back to David.

"No, actually, I'll be getting the place ready to sell."

"That's a pity; you'd be welcome here. Are you going to stay long enough for the Blessing of the Fleet?"

"I'd like to, but I'm afraid I have to get back to work. I've planned to be away for only a short time while I get things in order."

"You'll have to make it a point to come back for that then."

"I just might do that, Mary," David said, as he

reached into his back pocket for his wallet.

Mary raised her hand in protest and said, "Put that away, David; it's on the house."

"Thank you; I'll definitely have to come here more often."

"Hey, don't get use to it; I'm mean to my regulars," she said, smiling.

Out of the corner of his eye, David thought he noticed the old man watching him, but when he looked over in his direction, the old man continued to gaze into his glass of beer. *That's peculiar. I felt the guy looking at me*, David thought for a moment, but he then quickly turned his attention back to Mary.

"I want to thank you, Mary," David said, standing to leave.

"Hey, if there is anything I can do to help, just let me know, okay?"

"I'll do that, thanks."

As he emerged from the pub into the fresh air of the outdoors, he again strolled over in the direction of the docks. A small circular area included a flower garden and a couple of benches. This area's focal point was a fisherman's memorial. It consisted of a base of gray polished granite with a granite tablet etched with the names of those from Stuart Cove lost at sea. The area was well kept; it was obvious the garden had been given regular attention.

He bent down, leaning on one knee, so he could read all the names listed. One side listed names of individuals, and the other side listed the vessels' names and the dates. He looked closely at the names of the vessels: *My Lady* — July 14, 1952, *Echo II* — January 12, 1955, *Seahawk* — August 1, 1956.

"That don't tell the whole story."

David was so startled that he fell over on his other

knee. As he looked over his shoulder to see the old man from the bar standing over him.

"Where the hell did you come from?" David asked, still trying to recover. "You scared me to death."

The old man did not notice David's reaction.

"You Gina's nephew?"

So, he was listening to our conversation.

"Yes, I am," David said, rising to his feet.

At that, the old man turned and walked away toward Main Street. David was so taken aback by this that he just stood there for a moment. *I haven't met a guy quite so odd as that in a long time*, he thought, heading for his car.

Chapter Two

The warmth of the late morning was enough to wake David, as the sun poured into the bedroom. Opening his eyes, he looked over at the clock on the bedside table.

"Geez, its ten o'clock already," he said, slowly getting out of bed. *I seem to be sleeping later and later each morning.*

It was another beautiful day, hardly a cloud in the sky, a warm temperature, but not especially humid. David descended the narrow staircase and entered the kitchen.

Darn, I forgot to go to the store yesterday. I sure hope there's still some food left, he thought, opening the refrigerator. Inside was a half gallon of milk, three eggs, two beers, some grape jelly, half a stick of butter, half a package of sausages, and an end piece of bread.

"Looks like breakfast to me," David said aloud.

He pulled out a pan from the cupboard and began to cook breakfast. It was not long before the cottage filled with the smell of fresh coffee and sausages—particularly noticeable after he came back inside after retrieving the morning paper from the front yard. An area at one end of the kitchen included a small table and two chairs, where David settled down to read the paper and eat his breakfast. As he read about the local stories and events— "House of Delegates OKs Waterman Bill of Rights," "Matthew Earns Eagle Scout," "American Legion Post 325 Plans a Pork Dinner"—a feeling of wistfulness came over him. With almost a jolt, David paused, sat back, and realized that he was relaxing. He chuckled, as he found himself now analyzing this sudden realization.

I take days off at home. I eat breakfast and read the paper at home. Isn't that relaxing? Somehow it feels different here—very different. With that thought, he put

15

the paper down, threw the dishes in the sink, and proceeded to pour another cup of coffee.

The familiar sound of the seagulls drew him to the porch, where he sat in one of the rocking chairs, sipped his coffee, and gazed off in the direction of the creek. He began to think about the day before and the old fisherman at the bar.

What did he mean, "It doesn't tell the whole story"? Was he nuts, or did he want to tell me something? He pondered this thought for some time, as a gentle breeze moved slowly through the porch. His concentration was finally broken when he noticed a raccoon strolling across the backyard headed for the bulkhead.

I really do have work to do—grocery store, writing, getting this place ready. The day is already half gone and what do I have to show for it, he thought, as he went back into the house and began cleaning the kitchen. *If I'm not careful, I'm going to let this relaxing thing get the best of me.*

As he continued through the day—going to the grocery, organizing his aunt and uncle's belongings, and even writing a couple of pages of his novel—he found it difficult to stop thinking about the old man and his comment. He was drawn back to the memorial. *I wonder if he looks after that area, planting and caring for the flowers, polishing the granite, and keeping the dirt off the bricked walkway.* This area, as he clearly remembered, was an area looked after by someone who cared, not just a person applying routine upkeep.

It was late afternoon by the time David finally succumbed to his curiosity. He decided to return to the Fishhook Pub in search of the old man.

As he drove downtown, David felt a sense of urgency beginning the moment he chose to find this mysterious fellow, the decision he was struggling with all day. He was a little surprised at his determination, and it was this determination blinding him, as he drove through town. Unlike the day before when David was attuned to all the activities of Main Street, this afternoon, he did not notice the black cat sleeping among the many books in the bookstore's display window. He did not notice the young girls taking turns whispering into each other's ear, then giggling with delight. Instead, David began to question his pursuit, as he pulled into the pub's parking lot.

Hey, if he's not here, I'll just have a beer and go home. What's the big deal? Maybe I'm just looking for an excuse not to get my work done.

As he entered the pub, he was surprised to see how busy it was. Mary had her hands full. He approached the bar and noticed the old man was not there, at least not where he was sitting the day before. He looked around but figured this man would have claimed that same seat at the bar and looking anywhere else was pointless.

He remembered his pledge—*if the old man is not here, I'll have a beer and go home.* It was at that moment that Mary saw David. She reached in her pocket, pulled out a small piece of paper, and handed it to David. He took the note and quickly read it:

Meet me at the lighthouse at 5

There was no name on it, but he knew whom it was from. Just the same, he attempted to ask Mary. As Mary was steadily arguing with a group of unruly men, at the same time filling a fistful of mugs at the tap, she looked at David and nodded her head in the direction of the old man's seat, confirming his suspicion. Looking at his watch, he saw it was 4:40. With a new sense of purpose, he rushed out of the pub, got into his car, and headed for the lighthouse.

How the hell did he know I would come looking for him? This guy is even more mysterious than I first suspected, David thought, driving through town. On approaching the Ridge Port Bridge, the traffic began to slow.

Damn it, if you don't keep moving, we're going to get stuck here. A moment later, the bells rang as the traffic arms began their descent.

"See, I told you," David said aloud in frustration.

He could do nothing more but wait, as the massive road sections slowly raised. Rather than remain in the car, he joined others on the sidewalk to watch the line of sailboats maneuver single file through the opening, each blowing its horn twice in thanks, as they passed through.

The lighthouse was clearly visible in the distance. *I think I can now rule out just a nutty comment from a nutty old man; there's obviously more to it than that. Or is there? Maybe he is just a very creative nutty old man who gets a kick out of stringing along outsiders.*

David found himself again questioning his quest, but not enough to abandon his appointment. Instead, he glanced at his watch and worried he would not make it in time. The sound of the road sections descending interrupted David's thoughts. He rushed back to his car and started the engine, as the bells rang and the traffic arms rose. David could not help but look at the clock in the dashboard; it read 5:02.

Well, if I miss him, I miss him. This is crazy, anyway.

David tried to prepare himself for the high probability that he would not get there in time. He turned off the main road and proceeded toward the lighthouse, taking him out of the main stream of traffic. After a few

18

miles, trees lined each side of the road.

With the windows down, David could tell he was getting close because there was the slight smell of the bay in the air.

The lighthouse had been deactivated in the late fifties, and after some years of neglect, the Stuart Cove Historical Society took over the property and converted it into a museum. It had been many years since David had come here to visit with his aunt and uncle.

I don't even know when this place closes, he thought.

The clock in the dashboard read 5:12. Then, there on the right was a large wooden sign in the shape of a lighthouse and dwelling that read at the base, **Welcome to the Stone Ridge Lighthouse**. David turned onto the dirt road. Emerging from the tree line, road dust engulfed his car like a fog. He then entered the parking lot, where there were about ten cars. David realized, as he got out of his car, that the note had not been very specific as to where to meet. He looked around, but did not see his fisherman.

David heard a voice yell out, "You going to the lighthouse, sir?"

He turned and saw a short round man standing near a small white-and-blue shuttle bus. *The note did say meet me at the lighthouse.*

"Yes, I guess I am."

The man followed David onto the bus, jumped in the driver's seat, and started it up.

"It's been a busy day; we had a group of school kids come in from Scottstown Elementary."

"Is that so?" David replied, continuing to look around.

The bus began the short drive to the lighthouse, located at the end of the Point. As the bus pulled away from the parking lot, it entered an open grass area about a half-mile wide. The Point, surrounded by water, was slightly elevated on a rocky bluff.

"Hope you weren't planning on walking. Many people do when the weather is this nice, but since we close soon, I figured you probably want to get there faster."

"When do you close?"

"We close at half past six."

"Good, I was afraid you closed at five-thirty."

"You'd be cutting it a bit close if we closed at five-thirty," the bus driver responded with a smile.

"I was supposed to be meeting someone here, but I might have missed him," David said, as the bus pulled up to a small stone house standing a short distance in front of the lighthouse.

"Have you been here before?"

"Not in a long time."

"If you enter through the front door, there will be a small gift shop on the right. That's where you buy tickets. The tours run about every fifteen minutes. Hope you find your friend."

"Thanks," David said, as he stepped off the bus and looked around quickly. Even though only a few trees were scattered throughout the Point, the front of the house sat among mature Eastern hemlock that offered shade to the otherwise exposed area. He walked up the stone steps, entered the front door, and found himself in the entrance where an attractive young woman with long brown hair and hazel eyes greeted him.

"Hello. Welcome to the Stone Ridge Lighthouse. Will you be joining us on a tour today?" She was slender, slightly over five feet, and wore a mid-calf length skirt of thin flowered material swaying with every movement. Her pink V-neck top seemed to accentuate her slightly dark, even complexion.

"Actually, I was supposed to be meeting someone here, but I'm not sure where exactly."

"I haven't noticed any stragglers, but you're welcome to look around. If you walk straight through this way, you'll see a backdoor. Perhaps your companion is waiting out back."

"Thank you, you might be right. I'll take a look."

David was beginning to wonder again if he had been taken for a fool, as he headed down the hall to the backdoor. He opened the screen door and noticed a couple of picnic tables, but no sign of the fisherman. David descended the steps and there, a few yards in front of him, stood the lighthouse. He squinted, as the sun reflected off the bright white paint. Beyond the lighthouse, at the edge of the bluff, was a white picket fence. David took a quick walk around, but still no sign of the old man. He then decided to try one last place—the lighthouse itself.

As David reached out for the doorknob, the door swung open, and two young boys, laughing and ignoring all around them, almost knocked him over, as they exited.

"That was a close one." David heard a man's voice, but upon entering the darkened foyer, he could not at first see the person who spoke.

"Not scared of heights, are you?" the voice continued.

David could now see a tall man with a brown beard sitting behind a wooden counter to the left of the entrance.

"Actually, I was supposed to be meeting a gentleman here."

"There is a couple with their two children, a woman with her daughter, the parents of those two boys, but no gentleman touring solo, as I recall."

"Well, thank you," David responded, as he turned to leave the lighthouse.

The hell with this; I might as well take the tour, so I don't feel like a complete ass, he thought, heading back to the main house. *I just hope there's enough time left for that.*

"No sign of your friend?" The young woman asked, as David approached her in the hallway.

"No, I must have missed him, so I might as well take the tour while I'm here."

"You can buy your ticket from Millie. She's in the gift shop," the woman said, pointing in the direction of what appeared to be a parlor. Inside was a small fireplace against the outside wall with miniature lighthouses lined up on the mantel. The shop contained other lighthouse-related knick-knacks and locally made crafts strategically placed to avoid being knocked over by the strong breeze coming in through the open windows.

"Good evening, will you be touring the lighthouse?" Millie, a gray-haired woman in her sixties, had volunteered at the lighthouse for the past five years. She began her tenure after losing her husband. Her family had convinced her to get out and become involved in something. Millie noticed an ad in the local paper asking for volunteers to help out at the Stone Ridge Lighthouse and decided she would give it a try. She quickly fell into a routine and spent as much time there as she could. Millie was soon known as the mother of the light for her protective and *take-charge* attitude.

"Yes, I think I will take the tour."

"One ticket for you?" Millie asked from behind a small counter.

"Yes."

"Twelve seventy-five then," Millie said, as she tore a ticket from the ticket book and handed it to David.

"Thank you."

After collecting his change, David returned to the front foyer. "I guess you need this," and he handed the ticket to the young woman.

"Yes, thank you. My name is Claire. Have you been here before?"

"Not since I was about twelve years old."

"Good, then you're not at risk of a repeat performance," Claire said, as she motioned David into another parlor to the left of the entrance hall.

"We'll begin the tour here downstairs with the keeper's living quarters, then we'll move to the upstairs where there is a bedroom display and a small museum including an assortment of lighthouse memorabilia. Finally, I'll pass you on to Jim in the lighthouse itself. There, you'll proceed on a self-guided tour, up the light tower to the lantern room, if you're up to the challenge. The view is well worth the trip," Claire said with a smile.

The parlor was modestly decorated. David noticed the furniture seemed to be from assorted time periods. There was a fireplace on the far wall with a simple wood mantelpiece. The large plank wood floors sloped. The plaster walls were painted white and gave the false impression they were as uneven as the floorboards. Hanging on the walls were two paintings: one displayed a sailing vessel; the other, a family portrait.

Claire noticed David's attention to the oil paintings.

"Wonderful, aren't they? This one displays the *Master of the Seas*, one of the last clipper ships built by Randal Baines and launched in 1823 in Boston. This other painting is of the Stuart family, the town's namesake. Captain George Stuart, who served in the British Royal Navy from 1755 to 1768, is shown with his wife Mary and their two sons, James and Robert."

"Any connection with the lighthouse?" David

asked, examining the paintings closer.

"Yes, there certainly is. The clipper ship ran aground off the Point in 1829. Although a number of ships were lost in those early years, it was the *Master of the Seas* and its crew that finally convinced the government to build the Stone Ridge Lighthouse in 1831. As for the Stuart family, Captain Stuart's great-great grandson married the daughter of one of the early lighthouse keepers in 1867. You might have noticed the furniture dates to different periods. There is a reason for that," Claire continued.

"Since the lighthouse and home were manned from 1831 to 1956, the Stuart Cove Historical Society, who is currently responsible for this museum, could not decide what time period to reflect in the furnishings. Therefore, it was decided to include the whole span, as much as possible. We have collected various articles from past keepers and their families. The secretary you see is the oldest piece, having been here since the first family moved in. Several keepers have spent time at this desk, taking care of the necessary paperwork."

The secretary, standing against the inside wall, was a simple but solid piece of furniture made of cherry. The drop front was open, papers scattered, with the appearance that someone had just left behind unfinished business. The top bookcase contained a variety of timeworn books visible through the beveled glass. It concealed its age well, even though it exhibited its share of scratches. The grain of the wood gleamed in the filtered sunlight coming in through the curtains.

"This camelback loveseat dates to the early 1950s," Claire explained, pointing to a loveseat upholstered in a dark floral pattern. "Watch your step," she cautioned, as they moved into the adjoining dining room.

"The floor is a bit uneven."

"Yes, I noticed that."

"Over the years, keepers had an assortment of responsibilities. They had to keep the lenses and mirrors clean and wicks trimmed, carry heavy pails of oil, and wind and oil the clockwork mechanism. They had to whitewash the outbuildings every spring and keep on top of the paperwork, which included recording visitors and weather observations—all this in addition to the nightly watch to confirm the light was burning and the signal timing was accurate. With these many duties and responsibilities, there was not always time for the whole family to share dinner together, but during the longer days of the summer, chances of that would be better."

Next, they moved into the kitchen. The focal point was a large cast iron stove standing against the beige wainscot-paneled wall.

"This stove dates to the 1920s. Looking at it now, it's hard to believe it was a modern upgrade when it was brought in."

There was a small butcher-block table and two chairs alongside the inside wall. On the table were two coffee mugs, a plate of biscuits, and an oil lamp. Off the kitchen was a pantry. A curtain took the place of a door. It was pulled back to display the assortment of canned goods lined up along the shelves.

David noticed some type of list framed on the wall. "What's this?"

"That's a list of weekly food provisions allowed per man, as outlined in the *Instructions to Light-Keepers and Masters of Light-Vessels, 1902*."

"Interesting."

Next, they entered the hallway lined with black-and-white photographs.

"These are pictures of the many keepers who have lived here," Claire pointed out, as they slowly walked up the hall in the direction of the front entrance. "Upstairs is a small museum. Please watch your step. Sam will answer any questions you might have," she said, motioning David to ascend the stairs.

"Thanks."

As he reached the top of the staircase, David noticed two open rooms; one had a rope across the entrance. He walked up to the rope and looked inside. It was a bedroom containing a brass double bed, a dresser with washbasin, and a single wooden chair. He then proceeded to the opposite side of the hall and entered a large room. There inside were display cases and a number of artifacts. A slightly pudgy man with gray hair and reddish cheeks, who had been reading a book, stood up as David entered the room.

"Good evening."

"Hello, Sam."

"Please take your time looking around and feel free to ask me any questions."

"Thank you, I will," David responded, approaching a display case.

Inside was an old wooden box containing wicks and mantels. The display card read, "*Before electricity, most all navigational beacons used oil or kerosene lamps, the majority of which had wicks.*" Next to that was a tattered matchbox, wooden matches, and a torn matchbox wrapper. The display card read, "*Original government-issued matches.*" Moving down the case, David read the card next to a brass box, stating "*Brass-Boxed Cleaning Kit. Used by the keeper for polishing the lighthouse lens and brightwork.*" He especially noticed the next item. It appeared to be an old waterlogged piece of wood. The card read, "*Believed to be a plank from the ghost ship* Isidore." David hesitated here a moment.

"Have you heard about the sinking of the *Isidore*?"

Sam asked.

"No, I haven't."

"Would you like to?"

"Why, yes, I would."

"It was on November 26, 1842, when a crewman, Thomas King, dreamt about the ship *Isidore*, which was to set sail two days later. He dreamt it would be lost at sea. He pleaded with the captain, Ileander Foss, to release him from duty. The following night, another crewman had a dream. He dreamt of seeing seven coffins on the shore, one being his own."

Obviously, Sam enjoyed telling this story. With complete concentration, he continued, "Ignoring these premonitions, the captain set sail from York, Maine, and shortly after passing Cape Neddick Light, a terrible gale hit. The next morning, fragments of the ship began to wash ashore, along with seven bodies, including the sailor who had dreamt of the coffins. The captain's body was never found. As for Thomas King, he was not among the dead because he never left with the ship. He instead hid on shore, disobeying the captain's orders. There have been many sightings of the ghost ship *Isidore* carrying a phantom crew, all dripping wet."

"My, that's some story, and this is a plank from that ship?"

"That's what they say. There was even a song called *The Wreck of the Isidore* written about the sinking."

"I'll have to look that song up," David said, continuing to examine the various items, including a foghorn and a fourth-order Fresnel lens.

"Will you be touring the lighthouse?"

"Yes, I think I will."

"Good, just go downstairs and down the hall to the backdoor. The lighthouse is straight ahead; can't miss it," the man said with a grin.

"Thank you."

As he left the room, David passed a mannequin wearing a keeper's official jacket and cap. He then descended the staircase and saw Claire in the hallway.

"Ready to visit the lighthouse?"

"Yes, I am."

"Jim will take good care of you, and if you have any questions, don't hesitate to ask. He's our expert," Claire said, walking David to the back.

"Thanks," he responded, departing through the backdoor.

As the late afternoon turned to early evening, shadows were cast across the property, and the breeze seemed a bit cooler. Remembering his last encounter with the two boys, David entered the lighthouse a little more cautiously.

"Did you find your friend?"

"No, I didn't, so I decided to take the tour instead."

The spiral staircase took up most of the area, and Jim was tucked behind the small wooden counter.

"The height of this tower is 115 feet with a focal plane of 136 feet. Are you up for a climb?"

Walking over to the base of the staircase, David looked upward through the winding stairs, which had the appearance of a chambered nautilus half-shell.

"I think I can handle this."

"Since you're my last visitor, I'll join you; have to make my rounds before closing up."

They began their ascent.

"The first lighthouse in America was the Boston Light, built in 1716. This lighthouse, as I'm sure Claire told you, was built in 1831. Its light source was the second-order lens originally fueled by an oil lamp. In 1932, it went electric. Then, in July of 1956, it went dark, and the Black Sand Navigation Beacon took over the job. We don't know exactly how many keepers there were over the years, but we know two of them were women."

They continued their climb, spiraling against the tower's walls, occasionally passing a window or a landing where they could both rest a moment, as David inspected the various relics and photographs. Finally, they arrived at a room just below the lantern room. It appeared to serve the purpose of an office with a desk, a couple of chairs, a table with a coffee machine, and a table next to the desk with a radio on it.

"Haven't seen a radio like that in a while; my uncle used to have one," David said, approaching the table to look closer.

"That's an LEC Model LRK 3 channel receiver."

"We thought it was lost. Then, a few years ago, it was found when we were cleaning out a room. We decided to bring it back in here. Some people say it's haunted."

"Really, why do they say that?"

"Oh, I'll leave the ghost stories up to Sam."

They then proceeded up a narrow staircase to the lantern room. Here was the view that Claire had spoken of.

"This is a second-order lens—a beauty, isn't she?"

There, in the center of the room, was a massive prismatic lens standing more than six feet tall, sparkling in the evening sun.

"I'm certainly no expert, but I would have to agree with you—she sure is a beauty."

David circled the lens, his attention given equally to the amazing views and the inspection of the lens.

"You picked a good time of day to come up here."

"It sure is a sight to see. I'm glad I decided to stay."

Jim walked David back down the stairway—a trip

that went much faster than the trip up.

"I have a couple of things to finish up here; do hope you enjoyed your tour."

"Thanks, I thoroughly enjoyed it."

"Have a great evening."

As David walked toward the residence, he noticed someone sitting at one of the picnic tables. *Well, I'll be damned.*

"I didn't think you were here," he said, approaching the table. "As a matter of fact, I just finished taking the tour, just so it wouldn't be a wasted trip."

The old man looked up at David, but his face showed no expression.

"So, why did you call me out here, and what did you mean by yesterday's comment?" David asked, sitting adjacent to this mysterious old man.

"It is only names and dates," the old man replied.

"Okay, you have my attention."

"You a writer?"

Not many secrets around this town, David thought, as he answered. "Yes, why do you ask?"

"Because I have a story to tell."

"A story about the memorial?"

"A story about the *Seahawk*," the old man said in a quiet voice.

The old man moved in a little closer to David and asked, "Do you know that everything happens for a reason?"

This seemed like a somewhat odd question, but then, so was this whole conversation.

"I suppose it does," David responded.

David had to admit that the old man intrigued him a bit. He wanted to hear his story.

Chapter Three

"Year was 1954," the old man began, looking off to the distance.

"Dwight Eisenhower was president. As I recall, *Rear Window* with that movie star Jimmy Stewart was playing at the theater."

Where the heck is this going, David thought.

"*I Love Lucy* was all the rage," he continued. "I remember the year well; watchin' the World Series in color, the New York Giants and Cleveland, and ...," he paused. "A young man by the name of Danny was the keeper at the Stone Ridge Lighthouse."

The memories he held close for so long were finally coming forward in his story.

***

"I can't believe it—it's already 11:05. Sis is gunna kill me if I'm late for her wedding," Danny said to himself, putting the paintbrushes away. "Won't matter that I was painting these damn fences into the dark of night, and I've been at it since the crack of dawn this morning."

The ceremony was getting under way by the time Danny arrived. Mrs. Kessler was playing the wedding march, and Mr. Grimshaw had Helen by the arm, as they were proceeding up the aisle. Upon seeing this, Danny rushed in and tapped Mr. Grimshaw on the shoulder, whereby he graciously moved aside, and Danny slipped in his place, taking his sister's arm. She turned and looked at him angrily, as he smiled back at her, and they proceeded up the aisle. The church was packed, and all eyes were on them, as they approached the altar. It happened to be an unusually warm day for May, and Danny felt beads of sweat rolling down his face. Moments later, with his part in the ceremony completed, he was able to leave the altar and slip into the first pew, where Mrs. Rita handed him a handkerchief.

This church played a central role in the lives of all Stuart Cove's residents—the young had been baptized here, growing families had worshiped here, all had said good-bye to loved ones here, and now, it was the wedding of Helen and Scott that would be celebrated here. With his duty behind him, Danny could turn his attention to the moment. The spring flowers decorating the altar seemed to dance with the colorful rays of light coming in through the stained glass windows. As he watched the ceremony, his joyful mood turned a little downcast, as he thought about their parents and how they were not there to share this important day. Danny had tried to take on the role of father after he was lost to a boating accident seven years earlier, but when they lost their mother two years later to cancer, he was almost overwhelmed with a sense of responsibility. His sister then comforted him and assured him that everything would be okay, even though she was only twenty years old at the time. Their bond was very strong.

"I now pronounce you husband and wife. You may kiss the bride." As Helen and Scott kissed at the altar, the church rang out in cheer, bringing Danny's thoughts back to the joy of the occasion. He gave his new brother-in-law a hard slap on the back, as he and Helen made their way back down the aisle and out the front door of the church.

"I thought I hid the truck," Scott said, as he and Helen surveyed Scott's truck.

"Look at it; this is going to be embarrassing."

"Guess you didn't hide it as well as you thought."

"No, Mrs. Spear, I guess I didn't."

The 1945 Ford pickup had cans tied to the rear bumper and a handwritten sign in the small rear window, reading *"Scott & Helen."* Then, just as they started to collect themselves, the church doors burst open, and friends and family surrounded them.

***

Danny arrived back at the lighthouse with his arms full of grocery bags. He had felt a bit overdressed at the market, but since he was already out to attend the wedding, he thought it best to stop and pick up some supplies. Normally, Helen did the shopping, but Danny insisted she not concern herself with it. This took an argument from Danny because Helen felt he would not be able to get by alone while she was gone on her honeymoon, even though it would only be for three days. He had to admit, on arriving to an empty house, that it felt a bit odd not having her there. Then, he began to wonder about having both of them there—how different would it be? It was the most logical solution, though. With Scott tripping (out fishing for extended periods), Helen would otherwise be alone.

As he continued to put away the groceries, Danny's thoughts turned to work and all he had to do to make up for the short time he had been away from the lighthouse. He quickly went to his bedroom and changed out of his one good suit and back into his uniform.

The afternoon passed quickly, as Danny continued with his chores. He spent most of the time working on the diesel that powered the fog signal. By late afternoon, Danny was at the secretary, making log entries and completing government forms. Then, there was a knock at the door. He stopped and put down his pen. *I've been saved from the forms, at least for now*, Danny thought, walking to the entry hall. He opened the door to find Mr. Kessler standing there with a sullen look on his face.

"Shit, I almost forgot it." Mr. Kessler left the front steps and headed back to his car.

Danny stepped out and watching him, asked, "Jim, where 'ya going?"

A moment later, Mr. Kessler, in his plaid flannel shirt and his denim overalls, returned, holding a covered dish.

"This is from the missus; she doesn't think you can survive without Helen."

"Damn, Jim, you tell her it's very much appreciated, but she really didn't need to go to the trouble," Danny said, taking the dish and motioning Jim to follow him into the kitchen where he set the dish on the counter.

"Have a seat, Jim. Why don't ya join me for a cup of joe?"

Removing his baseball cap and placing it on the kitchen table, Jim replied, "It's four thirty in the afternoon. How about a beer instead?"

"Can't do that. I'm still on duty, but you're welcome to one."

"You're always on duty, Danny."

Danny reached into the fridge, brought out a bottle of Budweiser, and handed it to Jim. He then grabbed the kettle on the stove, gave it a shake to confirm it had a sufficient amount of water, set it on the stove, and turned up the flame.

"So, when they gettin' back from their honeymoon?"

"Sunday night some time," Danny responded, taking a stained off-white porcelain coffee mug from the cabinet and placing it on the table. He reached into a drawer, pulled out a bottlecap opener, and slid it across the table, at the same time falling onto the opposite chair across from Jim.

"Not much time for a honeymoon," said Mr. Kessler.

Mr. Kessler was a big man, emphasized in the small kitchen. His complexion permanently darkened by years at sea, had deep lines, with an expression of one who is tired. He had been a fisherman all his life. In his younger days, he crewed on the offshore draggers and was out for days at a time, keeping him away from his family. However, it was for his family that he fished. They went out in all weather, passing the time until they reached the fishing site. Then, the true work began. They unwound the ground cables from the large reel at the boat's stern. Then, as they dragged the net across the bottom, the water's resistance against the troll doors held the mouth of the net open wide to capture the fish. Hours later, when it was time to haul back, the captain stopped the vessel and put the winch into gear. The cables were brought back on board, as the men leveled them onto the drums, assuring that they coiled evenly. Once the troll doors were disconnected, the scissors and the troll wound back on the reel, and the heavy cot end was hoisted above the deck. As the cowbell was released, the cot end opened, and the load of fish was dumped on the deck. The men picked the deck with their spiked sticks, disregarding the trash fish and keeping the marketable ones.

In his later years, Mr. Kessler transitioned to a day boat, allowing him more time with his family. His day would usually begin at four a.m., arriving at the fishing site at dawn, at which time, they began the work of setting the gear. They usually arrived back at the dock around three in the afternoon, once there, they continued their work unloading their catch.

Mr. Kessler had been a good friend and shipmate of Danny and Helen's father. The Kesslers tried to check in on the brother and sister now and again, trying to fill the void as best they could after the loss of their parents. The couple admired their strength and resourcefulness.

"Scott's gotta get back. The *Seahawk*'s going out for a ten-day trip Monday morning," Danny said, spooning some instant coffee into the cup.

The kettle whistled. Danny got up, took it from the stove, poured the steaming water into the coffee cup, and returned it to the stove.

***

"Gentlemen, I'm afraid I've gotta kick you outta here; it's closing time," Claire said, clapping her hands as she passed the picnic table on her way to the lighthouse. The old man abruptly ended his story, got up from the table, and headed across the yard, catching David by surprise. David called out to him. "Hey, you haven't finished your story. What's your name?"

"Tomorrow, 1300, Black Sand Park," the man yelled over his shoulder, as he quickly departed.

"Where at the park?" David yelled after him, but the old man did not respond, as he disappeared behind the house.

"He did it to me again," David mumbled under his breath, getting up from the table. "He sure moves quickly for an old guy. He's practically stealth." Heading back to his car, David felt his phone vibrate.

"What'cha need, Russ?" he asked.

"Hey, David, I'm afraid I need some help with that story we were working on about the Board of Ed."

"What kind of help?" David asked; that story being

the furthest thing from his mind.

"I'm setting up my interviews, and I need to know if I should include Ms. Heather, 'cause if I do, that would probably change the approach to the story," Russ said.

"Of course, you should interview her. I thought we talked about that," David answered, obviously irritated, but realizing that he needed to guide Russ through the process, he added, "Look, Russ, how about I call you tomorrow morning about it?"

"Okay, I appreciate that," Russ responded.

David was now engaged in the old man's story, and he did not want to risk losing his train of thought, as he mulled over the events he had just heard.

Chapter Four

David was falling into a pattern of waking up much later than his previous custom of six a.m.; but knowing he had a ten o'clock meeting with Ellen, he woke up earlier, so he could have a leisurely breakfast and enjoy his coffee on the porch. It proved to be another fine morning. He had the windows open to capture the slight breeze coming off the water.

I can't believe how fast the time is going by. It's been a week already, and what do I have to show for it, David thought, cleaning up the kitchen. *I have to get this house ready to sell, work on my book, and ... what I didn't expect—hear about this bizarre story from an eccentric old man. He seems to be monopolizing most of my time lately.* This reminded him—*Shit, I almost forgot; I have to meet him at one o'clock today.* David considered canceling the appointment, but instead thought—*I'll give this story thing one more chance, but I can't spend my time here listening to this guy go down memory lane. Nope, I'm going to have to politely ask him to share his story with someone else who has time to kill. That's my plan.*

David spent the rest of the morning doing odds and ends and packing up a few more items. He was running late when he jumped into the shower to get cleaned up before Ellen was scheduled to arrive. He left the bathroom door slightly open, so he could hear the door.

I sure hope she's running late, David thought, attempting to hurry his shave without lacerating himself. *Who are you kidding; what realtor is late for an appointment to sell a house?*

Then, the knock at the door. In his haste, he broke the wall hook, as he grabbed his shirt.

"Damn, something else I'll have to fix," David said aloud, putting his shirt on at the same time he ran down the stairs to get the door.

"Hello, David."

"It's been a long time, Ellen. Please come in."

David stepped aside, as Ellen walked into the cottage, giving David a slight hug as she walked through the door.

"This IS a charming place, David," Ellen said, walking into the living room, very observant of her surroundings.

"Yes, it's not very large, but it does have its appeal," David responded.

"Can I get you something to drink? I made some iced tea."

"Yes, that would be nice. You don't mind if I wander to the back porch, do you?"

"No, not at all, I'll meet you there in a moment."

David went into the kitchen and poured two glasses of iced tea he had made the night before. Carrying the two glasses to the porch, he looked around and, surprisingly, did not see Ellen.

"Ellen!"

"Out here. I'm sorry, just thought I'd take a walk out to the dock."

"My aunt and uncle loved it out here, especially my uncle."

"I know they did," Ellen said, sipping her tea and looking over the water.

"Are you sure you want to sell this place? I certainly do not want to feel like I am pressuring you into that decision," Ellen said, as they walked back to the house.

"No, Ellen, you aren't. I've thought about it for a while. Yes, I do love it here, but I have made my life in

New York. I can always come back here to visit."

"If that's your decision, I can help you. What are your plans for the contents—an auction?"

As they walked back into the living room, David replied, "There is not a lot here and what is here is pretty worn. I'll probably donate what I can, have a few items moved to New York, and get rid of the rest. Of course, I have other chores I have to get done—some painting and repairs, like the bathroom hook I broke this morning. I have a company coming out to paint the exterior next week."

"Looks like you have your work cut out for you. When do you think you'll have the place ready to put on the market?"

"I have to go back to New York on July 11, so obviously, my target is to have it ready before then."

"You're going to miss the Blessing of the Fleet."

"Yes, afraid I will. Can I get you some more iced tea?"

"No, thank you, but I would like to look around some more, refamiliarize myself with the place."

"Go right ahead. I'll just put these glasses in the kitchen."

Ellen took a small spiral notebook out of her purse and began writing some notes as she went from room to room. David met back with her upstairs in the master bedroom.

"Do you have a price in mind, David?"

"Well, since I'm not from this area, I was hoping you could give me a recommendation."

"I can do that."

They continued to walk into each room, ending back in the living room.

"I'll go back to the office and start on the paperwork. Should be ready for you to review early next week. I'll give you a call. How does that sound?"

"Sounds great, Ellen. Thanks for coming by."

"I know you have a lot of work to do, but I hope you can find some time to enjoy yourself while you're here."

"I'll try to slip a little of that in," David said, opening the front door.

"Bye, David."

"Talk to you later."

David spent the next few hours repairing porch screens and boxing up items for charity.

***

Here I go again, meeting this guy, don't know his name, and don't know exactly where to meet him, David thought, pulling into the parking lot of the Black Sand State Park.

Not many open parking spaces were left on this Friday afternoon. The park was a popular place on the weekend for locals and tourists alike. Of the 625 acres of land, the park consisted of woods, ponds, and a small beach. There were pavilions with large picnic tables and a playground. The Black Sand Navigation Beacon stood about a quarter mile inland from the beach. Its steel structure seemed to be looking over the park.

Not knowing where to go, David just started walking toward the beach. He reached a rock jetty nearby and decided to sit there for a moment to determine what to do about finding this guy.

David looked out over the bay. There were large downy clouds in the sky with a deep blue backdrop. The shallow waves crashed against the rocks—a pure and rhythmic sound. Soon David closed his eyes to feel the sun's warmth and allow the sound to consume his thoughts.

"Follow me."

Startled, David's foot slipped off the rock and into the water.

"Quit doing that to me! Damn, now my foot is soaking wet. You are one weird guy, and how did you know where to find me?"

"Most people wander down here when they have no particular place to go," the old man responded and began walking down the beach.

David climbed off the rocks and had to sprint to catch up, his one wet shoe squeaking as he ran. Suddenly, he stopped.

"Hold on a minute."

The old man stopped and looked back at David.

"I'm not going any farther until you at least tell me your name."

"Name's Pierce," the old man said and continued walking.

"Okay, Pierce, where are we going?"

"Just goin' farther down the beach, less populated."

"So, did Scott get back from his honeymoon in time to catch the fishing trip?"

"Course he did, the *Seahawk* couldn't leave without her captain."

They walked down the beach, passing young children making sand castles in the wet sand. The children smiled with pride as they inspected their creations, unaware that later in the day, they would shed tears as the encroaching tide claimed their castles. Young boys braved the cold water, determined to use their new boogie boards, as their parents sat on their blankets watching all the activity. They continued their walk. The beach became narrow, encroached on by the woods. Then, they came to a small inlet. The beach itself was now covered with debris, both organic and artificial. No one else had ventured down this far. A few fallen trees lay in the sand, white and petrified after many years in the sun and water. Pierce stopped, grabbed a protruding log branch, and lowered himself onto the sand, leaning against the log. David stopped and sat on a log adjacent to him.

"I have to tell you; though, I'm sure you already know 'cause you seem to know about everything. I have a lot to do to get my aunt's place ready to sell. No offense, but I shouldn't be spending my time listening …"

Cutting him off in mid-sentence, Pierce said, "Know anything about fishin'?"

"No, can't say I do."

"There was a time when the fishin' round here was real good. It was so good; foreigners came and took our fish."

"I didn't think foreign countries could fish in American waters."

"Well, it changed in 1976 when those government guys passed some act there in Washington that changed the law, but it went on for years 'fore that, causin' our guys to go out for longer trips."

"So, that's why Scott was out for days at a time?"

"Yup."

"How did Helen deal with that?" David asked, as he removed his shoes and dug his bare feet into the sand.

***

"Ya talk to Helen 'bout us having to move outta here?" Danny asked, as he handed Scott the other half of the rag.

"Yea, I broke it to her this morning. Course she

44

knew it was comin' ever since they built that navigation beacon."

"You able to work something out with the Coast Guard?"

"Yea, they're gonna keep me on. I'll be workin' out of the Port Evens station. I signed the papers to rent the Allen cottage," Danny suddenly divulged.

With a surprised look, Scott responded, "When did you find time to get that done without anybody knowin'?"

"I have my ways."

"That's a nice place. Kinda big, though, isn't it?"

"I got it so you and Helen could move in with me."

Scott stopped polishing and turned to Danny.

"Now, you should have talked to us about that first, Danny. We've taken advantage of your generosity long enough, brother-in-law. What's it been, two years?"

"There abouts, I guess," Danny said, continuing to polish the brass.

"I think it's time we got our own place."

"What about Cynthia? She's only a year old. What's Helen going to do when you're out tripping?"

"She'll manage fine, Danny. We'd still be in Stuart. There's the Kesslers and you to check up on her. You act like I'm the only captain with a young kid."

Danny put the rag down and walked out onto the gallery. Looking out across the bay, he replied, "You know I worry about my sis, always have."

Scott joined him and crossed his arms on the rail. "I know that, but you're gunna have to let go. She's my wife, and we need to be on our own."

"I understand; just need to get used to the idea, Scott. Ya know, as many times as I come out here, I just never get tired of this view."

"Know what 'cha mean."

The men returned to the lantern and commenced with the polishing.

**

"Scott radioed in, should be at the cove in about thirty minutes. Now you ain't planning on meetin' him at the wharf, are ya?" Danny asked Helen, as he stood in the kitchen, water dripping from his rain gear, creating puddles on the floor.

"Ya know I always meet him when he comes home, Danny. Now, get back to your lighthouse. You're making a mess in here."

Helen made a personal commitment to herself when she became Scott's wife that she would always be there at the wharf when he left for a trip and when he returned, no matter what.

"I can't leave the light, or else I'd go get him."

"I know you would. Now, get the hell outta here."

Danny went out the backdoor, pulling the tip of his hood down over his face, as he headed out into the pouring rain toward the signal house.

It had been a hot day in July, collecting into a powerful afternoon storm. The sky had darkened to be lit up by the flash of lightning, followed closely by cracks of thunder.

Helen put on her raincoat, wrapped Cynthia in a blanket, and, grabbing an umbrella from the umbrella stand, ran out to the truck. The wind promptly caught the umbrella and popped it inside out, making it useless.

With his work done in the signal house, Danny was on his way to the lighthouse when the truck headlights caught his attention. *That sister of mine is one hardheaded lady. She don't ever listen to me.*

The wipers were barely keeping the pounding rain

off the windshield, causing Helen to maintain a slow pace.

"Your daddy's gunna be real happy to see you. You know you're Daddy's little girl," Helen said to Cynthia, trying to keep herself calm, as she had to drive around small dead branches that had fallen onto the road from the surrounding trees.

"Yup, he's gonna be real glad to see you."

Every once in a while, the rain would begin to dissipate, just to be followed by a downpour. At that slow pace, it took twice as much time as usual to get to the Ridge Port Bridge. Helen continued her drive through town where the streets were deserted, then down to the wharf where she stopped and parked. It was difficult to see through the rain. Helen did not think she saw the *Seahawk*, so she stayed in the truck and waited. She continued to wait for what seemed like an eternity, getting more worried by the moment, chatting nonstop with Cynthia, who had since fallen asleep. Then, as sudden as it had started—the rain stopped. Helen got out of the truck and walked down the wharf. There it was, in the distance, the *Seahawk*, making her way home.

By the time they got back to the lighthouse, the sun was back out, and the only evidence of the storm were some puddles and a few small branches scattered about the ground.

"Sure is good to be back eatin' your cooking, honey. I was getting mighty tired of Roy's attempts," Scott said, joining Danny and Helen at the dining room table.

"When you g'tting' that new cook you interviewed?" Helen asked, as she fed Cynthia another spoonful of cereal."

"'Spect he'll be ready for our next trip."

"And when's that?" Helen asked.

"I told 'ya I'd be here for the Blessing of the Fleet, so we're going out right after that."

"Good," Helen responded with a satisfied look on her face.

"Pull in a good catch?" Danny asked, helping himself to the mashed potatoes.

"'Bout twenty-two hundred pounds. Not as good as last trip, but not bad."

They continued their dinner, talking about the fishing trip and the chores that had to be done over the next few days.

"That was a fine dinner," Danny said, jumping up from his seat and leaving the room.

"If it was so fine, why ya running out in such a hurry?"

"Just a minute," Danny called back.

Danny returned, carrying a large item wrapped in a sheet.

"What the hell is that?" Scott asked.

"Watch your language around Cynthia," responded Helen.

"Here, it's for you two—a gift. Open it."

Helen's eyes were wide. With a smile on her face, she asked, "What's the occasion? It's not our anniversary."

"It's a housewarming present."

"A housewarming present," Helen said, helping Scott unwrap the large item to reveal its contents.

"A painting," Helen said with excitement in her voice.

"That's nice," Scott said.

"Nice? It's more than nice. This is a painting of the *Master of the Seas*, the last clipper ship built by Randal Baines.

"You know your history, sis."

"I remember when you got this, Danny. You picked it up from that antique place. The guy there didn't know what he had, thought it was just some old boat picture." She stopped and looked straight at Danny. "We can't take this."

"Sure you can, 'cause I'm giving it to ya."

"We haven't even moved out yet," Scott added.

"Yea, well this is my way of saying ya have my blessing. Now take it."

Helen handed the painting to Scott and gave her brother a big hug.

"Thanks, Danny, this means a lot."

"It's nothin. Yu gonna watch *I Love Lucy* with me?" Danny asked and walked out of the room.

***

Life settled down into the two-keeper routine.

"So, you and Helen find a house yet?" Danny asked Scott, as they worked in the signal house.

"Maybe. We're looking at that place on Pennington Street, near where Roy lives."

"Not a bad place and close by," Danny replied.

"We decided to wait until I get back from the next trip, and then make the decision."

"You have time. The Coast Guard wants me to stay here until August 24. I'll be helpin' with the decommission. No problem with you all stayin' till then. Maybe they're closing this place just in time. Seems I'm spendin' an awful lot of time keepin' this diesel going."

"Ya right about that, Danny."

They continued working into the late afternoon.

***

Every conversation taking place in Stuart Cove over the last few weeks seemed to revolve around the upcoming Blessing of the Fleet festival. The town was well aware of the tradition, but had not yet held the event themselves. As the weekend approached, every family in town was busy preparing for the event. Helen was up early Saturday morning, the first day of the festival, making apple pies and potato salad.

"Do I smell apple pie with my breakfast?" Scott asked, coming into the kitchen.

"Yup, but you're only getting breakfast, no apple pie yet."

"How many people you planning on feedin'?" Scott asked, pouring himself a cup of coffee.

"You can never have too much apple pie," Helen responded in a cheerful tone.

"I'm gunna have to catch up with you all at the park. Roy and Chip are coming by. We have some work to do on the boat."

"You sure you're going to be done in time?"

"I'm sure. Besides, the guys wouldn't miss this—their wives won't let 'em."

Danny entered the kitchen with Cynthia in his arms. "I think this little girl wants some apple pie."

"Are you crazy?" Helen asked. Helen took Cynthia and gently placed her in her highchair.

"Guess I can drive in with ya, Helen. Since they turned off the light, I don't have to be here at dusk," Danny said, pouring himself a cup of coffee.

"You're sad about that aren't ya, Danny?" Helen asked.

"Yea, I guess."

"Well, the good thing is you can help me carry all this food," Helen said, regretting her last comment.

The two men sat at the small kitchen table eating

their breakfast as Helen continued preparing her salad and feeding Cynthia.

***

"Afternoon, Mr. Kessler," Helen yelled out the truck window.

Mr. Kessler was getting a blanket out of his car, as they pulled up.

"Where's Scott?"

"He's comin'," Danny responded. "He had some work to do on the *Seahawk*."

They parked, got out, and as Helen reached for the baby carriage from the truck bed, Mr. Kessler stopped her.

"Let me get that, Helen."

"Why, thank you, Jim."

With Mr. Kessler's help, they were able to get all the food and supplies to the picnic area. Every family of Stuart Cove was in attendance. The barbecues at the pavilion were all in use, cooking hamburgers and hotdogs. The kids were playing games, and the adults were enjoying the company of friends. Scott showed up a short time later to join in the celebration. Mayor Lynn addressed his town, welcoming everyone to the festival and reminding everyone why they were there—to remember those who had lost their lives at sea and to pray for a safe and bountiful season. Father Daniel led everyone in prayer before dinner. As the afternoon turned into early evening, a local band played and the festivities continued.

The following day, the township gathered at St. Margaret's Church for a special Mass dedicated to the lost fishermen. The altar was decorated with fishnets, shells, boat models, wreaths, and American flags. It was a moving ceremony, especially for the families who had personally lost loved ones. As Helen sat with her family and friends, she was reminded of the danger Scott faced in his profession—a thought she tried very hard to bury deep in her emotions. The somber mood of the service was still evident as the families exited the church. Even the children were quiet, reacting to their parents' emotion.

*　*　*

By early afternoon, children with balloons and cotton candy were joined by others lining up along Main Street. The parade had begun. The high school band was there in their bright blue-and-white uniforms. The mayor and his wife were driven in his black Cadillac convertible decorated for the occasion. There were floats carefully crafted into the shapes of trawlers and dinghies. An especially large replica carried the Princess of the Fleet, the young Miss Betty Taylor. Also included in the parade was a float carrying a statue of Saint Andrew surrounded by fresh flowers. The men from the local fire department proudly carried their banner, followed by the fire truck with its lights flashing. As the end of the parade continued down Main Street, the crowd followed, ending at the waterfront where everyone dispersed in all directions around the docks and onto the boats for the blessing.

*　*　*

Helen was always a little melancholy before Scott's fishing trips, but it was especially prevalent before this trip. She was not sure why, but assumed it was in reaction to the previous weekend and the blessing of the fleet. She had to be strong, though, for herself and their daughter, so she tried never to openly show this concern and kept her forlornness to herself.

They arrived at the dock in the mid-afternoon. The plan was for the crew to get underway and reach the fishing area by early the next morning.

Scott grabbed his duffle bag from the truck bed and came around to meet Helen, as she stood on the wharf holding Cynthia close to her chest. The seagulls were calling and flying overhead. There was much activity at the wharf—boats coming in and others getting ready to go out.

Scott yelled to Roy who was helping load supplies onto the *Seahawk*. "Our cook show up?"

"Yea, captain, he did. He's down below," Roy yelled back.

Turning his attention back to Helen, "You okay, honey? Is something wrong?" Scott stood in front of Helen, put down his bag, and looked into her eyes.

"I'm fine," Helen said, quickly snapping out of her stupor. Don't ya dare worry about me. You gotta worry about that crew of yours. Now, did ya forget anything?" Helen asked, again taking control of the situation.

"Ya ask me that every time. Do I ever forget anything?"

"No, I guess ya don't," Helen responded.

Cynthia interrupted them by making her special cooing sounds.

"She wants to say good-bye to her daddy," Helen said, turning Cynthia around, so she could see her father.

"Ya be a good little girl for your mommy, and you be a good little girl too," Scott said, putting his arm around Helen and Cynthia.

"I love you two, ya know that, right?"

"Yes, we do," Helen responded.

Scott looked deep into Helen's eyes for a moment. He gently took her chin, brought her to his lips, and kissed her.

She looked back into his eyes. "I love you."

He grabbed his duffle bag, walked down the dock, and as he reached the *Seahawk*, turned and waved to his family.

***

Life back at the lighthouse was getting chaotic, Danny was busy packing up whatever property could be used at other lighthouses, making arrangements for an auction, and getting the remaining items ready for storage there at Stone Ridge.

"I think I'm gunna bid on some of this furniture when we have that auction," Danny said to Helen, as they sat at the kitchen table eating lunch.

"You and Scott decide on that house yet?"

"Scott's due back Wednesday, says he'll decide then, but I think we're going to do it. Besides, we don't have much time. We have to move outta here."

"You know you all can come stay with me," Danny said, sipping his coffee.

"Scott told you he didn't want to do that," Helen responded.

"I know; just a temporary thing, till ya find a place, that's all."

"We've been talkin' about that house a lot. I really think Scott's already decided, but he wants me to want it too."

"And do ya?"

"Yes, Danny, I think I do. As a matter of fact, I'm getting a little excited about it. This will be the first time I've been away from you, though." Helen paused, "What about you?"

"I'll be fine. Don't ya worry about me. You have your own family to look after now. Maybe you'd like to bid on some furniture too."

"Maybe we will."

"You're gonna miss this place, aren't ya, Danny?"

"Yea, I've looked over this place and guided the boats for more than six years," Danny said, looking down into his cup of coffee. "But ya know, a lot of the lighthouses are either working on their own or being replaced by those new devices," Danny continued.

"Yea, but it's still sad," Helen said.

"Gotta move on sis," Danny said, getting up from the table.

"I suppose you're right," she responded, going into the living room to continue her chores.

"Danny, come in here."

"I've got to get back to work, sis."

"Right now."

Danny, hearing the alarm in her voice, immediately met her in the living room.

"What's wrong?" he asked.

"Listen," she said, looking at the radio.

"There's been a report of a strong storm off the east coast. We'll be keeping an eye on this. Now for our local weather."

Helen turned to Danny, "Why didn't you tell me about this?"

"Didn't want to worry you. Besides, I've talked to Jim 'bout it, and he thinks it will move farther north and back out to sea. They say it's not moving very fast, so we expect if it does come this way, it won't be until after Scott's back home."

"Did you consider the fact that Jim might be wrong? Those weather guys don't always get it right, ya know."

"Calm down; I've relied on his reports since we've been here."

"I hope you're right. Promise me you'll let me know right away if anything changes."

"I promise. Now, get back to packing up those boxes, and quit thinking 'bout it."

Helen felt better after the reassurance from her brother.

Over the next few days, though, the tension in the house became unbearable. The storm was still moving slowly, and it would not commit to a more predictable course.

***

It was a beautiful day with blue skies and a gentle breeze. Helen was working in the garden when she heard the Kesslers drive up. She stood up, took her gloves off, and approached the car as they were getting out.

"Mr. and Mrs. Kessler, how nice to see you. What brings you this way?"

Mrs. Kessler rushed over to Helen and gave her a hug.

"Oh, honey, you must be worried to death."

Helen fought the urge to break down in Betty's arms. "Please come in. I have to check on Cynthia. She should be waking up from her nap about now."

The Kesslers followed Helen inside where they could hear Cynthia crying upstairs.

"Please make yourself at home while I go get her. I'll be right back."

"Ya know you might be making things worse by coming here and making a fuss, Bet," Jim said to his wife, as he paced the floor.

"Nonsense, Jim, she needs our support right now

and quit pacing the floor. You're making me nervous.

"Sorry 'bout that," Helen said, entering the room with Cynthia in her arms.

"Can I get you anything? Some iced tea?"

"That'd be lovely, dear, but let me help you."

The ladies soon returned to the dining room where Mr. Kessler joined them at the table.

"Hear you're going to buy that house on Pennington," Mrs. Kessler remarked.

"No secrets round here," Helen responded. "Actually, we haven't decided yet. We're going to make that decision when Scott gets home."

At that moment, Danny came running into the house from the backdoor. "Helen, where are you?" He stopped suddenly at the entrance to the dining room when he saw everyone at the table.

"What is it, Danny?" Helen asked, jumping up from her chair with a startled look on her face.

"It's the storm; it seems to have changed course. It's headed in this direction."

"Scott's not coming home until day after tomorrow," Helen responded.

"That's the thing. Last I heard from the *Janet*, Scott decided to come home early to try and avoid the storm."

"Someone's gotta get a hold of Scott," Helen yelled.

"We're trying."

"Where's the *Janet* now?"

"They're expected back in port any time."

Jim quickly got up and took Cynthia from Helen's arms. Helen could not hold back her emotions any longer. She finally broke down, as Betty wrapped her arms around her, trying her best to comfort her.

"The Coast Guard's on alert, and we're trying to reach him. I have to get back to the radio and monitor the

57

calls."

"Your light's been turned off, hasn't it?" Mr. Kessler asked.

"Yea, they disconnected it; couldn't turn it back on if I wanted to. The navigational beacon is on at Black Sand, though."

"I don't think they should've turned this light off; it's been guiding our ships for more than 100 years." Mr. Kessler said with anger in his voice. "That damn beacon thing better do its job," he continued, as Danny ran out of the room and out the backdoor. Before he reached the lighthouse, he stopped and looked out over the water— flocks of seabirds were flying to shore.

"How could this happen? They said it wasn't gunna come here, said it was gonna go back out to sea," Helen said between sobs, as the fear and tension finally came to the surface.

The gentle breeze was suddenly changing to a strong wind, and clouds were moving in.

"Everything's going to be fine, honey. Scott's a top-notch captain. He'll get his crew home; don't you worry," Betty said, still holding Helen in her arms.

"We're going to stay right here with you," Mr. Kessler said.

"Don't you have to get home?" Helen asked, trying to collect herself.

"Nope, here's where we have to be," Jim said, going into the living room to turn on the TV. "Let's see what they have to say 'bout this."

They all collected around the TV set to see what the local news channel was reporting.

"I'm going out and get things secure," Jim said.

"Be careful, dear," Betty called after him, as he went out the front door.

As the afternoon wore on, the skies darkened, and it

began to rain. It started lightly, but as night fell, it turned into a downpour.

"Where do you keep your candles, honey?" Betty asked while Helen rocked back and forth in the rocking chair trying to comfort Cynthia.

"They're in the drawer of the hutch in the dining room."

"It won't be long before we lose electricity, I'm sure. Betty said, collecting the candles.

"And where are the matches?"

"Kitchen."

Now, with a feeling of foreboding, Helen took Cynthia upstairs to their bedroom. As she approached the window, the lights went out. Holding Cynthia close, she looked out into the blackness, hoping to see the *Seahawk*. As she strained to catch sight of a vessel, the flashes of lightning allowed a glimpse, a hope of something out there, but then at next strike, it was gone.

"The barometric pressure is still dropping," Danny said, as he and Jim sat in the lighthouse, listening to the two-way radio.

"It's bad out there."

"Yea, I feel pretty damn helpless without my light," Danny responded. "Wish to hell they'd waited longer before turning her off," he continued.

"I better check on the ladies. You gonna be all right out here?"

"Jim, this has been my job for the last six years. Question is—you gonna be able to get back to the house? It's damn bad out there now."

"I'll be fine."

As Danny listened to the sound of Jim's footsteps becoming faint, as he descended the staircase of the lighthouse, he noticed the wind was entering every minute opening and swirling around the inside of the

59

structure. The gravity of the situation at that moment fully sank in.

His attention was then suddenly averted to the radio. He heard a distress call.

"Mayday—mayday—mayday—mayday—mayday—mayday. This is the fishing vessel Seahawk, our coordinates ...." Static interrupted the alert. "... we are taking on water ..." more static, "... need help."

***

Pierce abruptly stopped his story.

"I take it the date was August 1, 1956—the same date listed on the memorial?" David asked.

The old man got up, brushed the sand off his pants, and began walking away.

"Where are you going? Is that the end?"

David had to quickly put his shoes back on. As he did so, he called out to Pierce, who was walking away. "Hey, Pierce, are you gonna answer me?"

Pierce stopped, turned to David, and said, "That memorial—it doesn't tell the whole story."

"Yea, you told me that before. So what's the whole story?"

"At the jetty, tomorrow, 1500." And the old man turned and continued walking.

Chapter Five

David arrived at their meeting spot at exactly three o'clock as arranged, but he did not see Pierce. After fifteen minutes, David decided to walk around to stretch his legs and see if perhaps he went to a different location nearby. He wandered over to the playground and watched a young boy and girl chasing each other, sliding down a tall sliding board, screaming with delight as the other would come *almost* close enough to be tagged. This kept David entertained for a short time, until he noticed the mother sitting on a nearby bench watching him with a very seething look on her face. David decided he better move on.

After continuing his walk around the park, he looked down at his watch—3:30. *Okay, I give up*, David thought, *this guy really enjoys stringing me along.*

David left the park and headed for the hardware store to pick up some supplies, including a hook to replace the one he broke the day before. On reaching Johnson's Hardware, he decided to stop in first at the Fishhook Pub to see if the old man was instead hanging out at the bar.

As soon as he entered the pub, he noticed the atmosphere was not the usual upbeat place, with loud conversations and arguments; it was instead downcast. Mary was at the bar quietly washing some glasses. David hesitated and, feeling a bit uncomfortable, asked Mary if she had seen the old fisherman who had given him the note. Mary, holding back tears, responded, "Do you mean Danny?"

So, he is Danny, David thought. As he was collecting his thoughts and quickly putting all the pieces of the puzzle together, he said, "Yes, Danny."

Mary broke down and had to walk away. A bartender who overheard the exchange took Mary to a booth and spoke to her for a few minutes before returning. "Danny died in his sleep last night; a friend found him this morning."

David slowly lowered himself onto the barstool and, in a moment of shock, said aloud, "Everything happens for a reason."

"Excuse me," said the bartender, looking at David with a concerned look on his face.

"Danny told me that—I didn't even know that was Danny."

"Can I get you something to drink, buddy? You gonna be okay?"

"Yes, thank you, I'll be fine—just need a minute and a glass of water."

"Coming right up," the bartender said, grabbing a glass, filling it with ice and water, and placing it in front of David.

"You need anything else, you let me know."

"Thanks," David said, taking the water.

"I just can't believe it," David said under his breath.

He sat there while quiet conversations went on around him. He thought about Danny's story and all the questions he had wanted to ask.

So, everything happens for a reason, and what would that reason be, old man?

David left the pub and returned to the cottage.

Chapter Six

All of Stuart Cove, including the elderly Helen Spear, who was helped by her daughter Cynthia and Cynthia's husband Steven, attended the service held for Danny Pierce. St. Margaret's Church was overflowing. After the service, a reception was held in the fire station banquet hall. David was very interested in meeting Helen, but as he gave her his condolences, he thought it best not to mention the conversations he had with her late brother. His impression of her at this time in her life was that of a woman who had carried a very heavy burden. David could not help but feel sorry for her. He was glad to see that friends and family surrounded her.

David moved about the room conversing with old friends and making some new ones. He helped himself to the buffet table, sampling the tuna salad sandwiches and the homemade coleslaw.

"Glad to see you could make it."

David looked up from his plate and saw Claire, the young woman who had given him the tour of the lighthouse.

"It's Claire, right?" David responded, as he quickly put the sandwich down and found a place to get rid of the plate.

"Yes, and this is my boyfriend Tyler."

David reached out for a handshake, as he finished chewing his sandwich. "Hi, Tyler, glad to meet you."

"Had you known Danny for long?" she asked.

"No, actually, I just met him about a week ago."

"I saw you talking to him at the lighthouse. I assumed you had known him for while."

David leaned in closer and in a quiet voice said, "I hope you don't mind my saying this, but I found Danny, shall I say—interesting."

Claire smiled. "We loved Danny, but yes, he was unique."

David stepped over to the nearest table that had some empty seats and invited the two to sit. "When you saw us together the other day, he was telling me a story."

David sat in the chair next to Claire. "He was telling me a story about the *Seahawk*."

The expression on Claire's face suddenly changed. She looked surprised.

"He told you about the *Seahawk*?"

"What's the *Seahawk*," Tyler broke in.

Claire explained, "The *Seahawk* is the name of the fishing boat Danny's brother-in-law owned. It was lost at sea during a storm." Then, turning her attention back to David, "I can't believe he talked to you about that."

"What's weird is that, as he told me the story, he didn't tell me his name was Danny. I thought his name was Pierce talking about a guy named Danny."

"Of course, that was before my time," Claire began, "but being a native of Stuart Cove and especially working at the lighthouse, I know a lot of the history, which certainly includes Danny. He has never talked to anyone about that evening. People said he felt responsible for what happened because he didn't have the light on."

"But that wasn't his fault," David responded. "The Coast Guard turned it off, and besides, they had the Black Sand Beacon turned on."

"Yes, that's true, but I don't think that changed how he felt."

"What did Danny and his sister do after the accident?" David asked, hoping to fill in some of the missing pieces.

"Danny became a fisherman. They say when he was out fishing, he was really keeping an eye out for his brother-in-law. Helen never remarried. She lived with Danny for a short time but ended up getting a job and getting her own place. It's said her relationship with her brother changed after the accident. Neither one of them was really the same after that."

"Thing is," David cut in, "he didn't finish his story."

"I don't understand. He told you how the *Seahawk* was lost at sea?"

"Yes, he told me about that evening, getting the mayday call, but that's where he stopped. He said, and I quote, 'That doesn't tell the whole story.' We had an appointment to meet the next day to continue the story, but he passed away that evening."

"Interesting, but what else is there to say about it?" Claire responded, looking a bit puzzled.

"I'll have to say, I'm intrigued; I'm thinking about writing a human interest story about this."

"Really?" Tyler responded.

"I work for a newspaper in New York. Actually, I'm here to take care of my aunt's property since she passed away."

"As you might know, there aren't many secrets in this town. We knew that," Tyler said.

"You did, and what else do you know about me?" David asked, now curious and a little surprised by his comment.

"We know you're going to sell your aunt's house and that you're here until early July to get it ready. Then, you're going back to New York."

"Well, you're wrong," David said with smile. "It so happens I was called back early to take care of some things at work. I'll be leaving here in a few days. I'm going to have to put off the house thing until the end of July, assuming I can return then."

"Oh," Claire said, "can't say the local talk is always accurate."

"So, are both of you Stuart Cove natives?"

"I am, but Tyler isn't. He moved here from Colorado."

"That's a long way," David said.

"And, as you know, I volunteer at the Stone Ridge Lighthouse."

"Yes, I knew that much."

"We both work for the Coast Guard. Tyler's full-time, and I'm part-time because I'm also going to school."

"So, you live here in town?"

"I share a small house outside of town with my friend Kay, and Tyler has a place closer to Port Evens."

"David," Ellen said, approaching the table.

"Hi, Claire, Tyler. David, I just wanted to let you know I have the papers done; it'll wait until you come back. Just give me a ring when you know when that'll be."

"I'll do that, Ellen. I expect it'll be the end of July some time, but I'll call you."

"Thanks, and sorry, I didn't mean to interrupt."

"That's fine," Claire responded. "We have to get going, anyway. David, thanks for the conversation, and good luck with your story."

"How's your book coming along?" Ellen asked, as Claire and Tyler left the table.

Half listening to Ellen, David responded, "Oh, I guess it's coming along."

On David's return to New York, he found himself pining for those quiet mornings—drinking his coffee, looking out over the water from the screened porch. Within a week, though, he was back into the long days and fast pace of work.

Lance, who had been staying at David's condo while he searched for his own apartment, was in the kitchen cooking dinner when David came home from work.

"Hey, smells good, whatcha cooking?" David asked, walking into the kitchen while loosening his tie.

"Thought I'd make some lasagna."

"Great, I'm starved."

David went to his bedroom to change out of his suit and into his regular attire—jeans and a tee-shirt.

As David walked back toward the living room, Lance suddenly reached his hand out from the kitchen, blocking his way. "Here's a beer, man."

"Thanks," David said, grabbing it on his way.

David's apartment was of average size but large by New York standards. It was a one-bedroom, with one bath, a living room, and a small kitchen. He got it for a good price because the guy he bought it from had recently divorced and was unable to make the mortgage payments on his own. He purchased the furniture at the same time, so everything fit nicely in its place and was coordinated. The colors were dark, mostly black and silver, reflecting a masculine style—screaming "bachelor pad."

"You think you could have put this sofa bed back together? I can never sit here," David yelled toward the kitchen.

"Sorry, guy, I was in a hurry to get to work this

morning," Lance said, joining him in the living room. "So, did you bring up that *Seahawk* story with Brian yet?"

"Yes, I did, and he wasn't too kind to the idea. He didn't think that type of story was interesting enough."

"So, you're not going to write it?"

"Oh, I am; had to talk him into it, though. Pisses me off I had to fight about it. Course now, I have to make it a killer story—make my point."

"Yea, I guess you do," Lance responded.

"I have a resource I can contact for information on the lighthouse, though."

"Make a point, killer story ... I know what your real motivation is—Claire, you sly dog."

"Hey, I'm a professional. I still have a point to make, and I will."

"I'm sure you will."

"And what kind of guy do you take me for? I'm not going to make a move on Tyler's girlfriend," David said, dialing the phone.

"Hello, is this Claire?"

"No, it's Kay. Hold on, I'll get Claire."

"This is Claire."

"Hi, this is David. I hope you don't mind my calling you. I got your number from Ellen."

"Hi, David, are you back in town?"

"No, I'm still in New York. You remember my saying I was going to do a story about the *Seahawk*?"

"Sure do."

"Well, I could use some help with lighthouse research, especially your lighthouse."

"I'd be happy to help you with that."

"Great, looks like I'm going to be able to get back there on the twenty-eighth. Can we plan to meet after that?"

"You know the Blessing of the Fleet is the thirty-first. You're going to that, aren't you?"

David actually forgot about the Blessing of the Fleet, but he could not let Claire know that.

"Sure, I'm going."

"Have you attended a Blessing?"

"No, I haven't."

"Well, then, why don't you join Tyler and me for the Blessing? Give me a call when you get into town. We'll set up a time and place."

"Sounds good, Claire, and thanks for agreeing to help me out with this."

"My pleasure, so happens lighthouse history is a passion of mine."

"Looks like I have a research date," David said after he hung up the phone.

"Well, aren't you the professional," Lance responded.

***

David felt a sense of relief as soon as he stepped back inside the cottage. *Good to be back*, he thought.

David spent the next few days getting back to his chores. He was finally seeing some real progress on the place. The house's exterior had been painted while he was in New York, and he had a date scheduled for an auction.

A number of people were already at the Black Sand State Park when David arrived to meet Claire and Tyler.

"David, over here," Claire shouted from the direction of the pavilion.

"Great to see you again," David said, approaching Claire, who was with a small group of friends.

Claire introduced David to her friends and

explained that David was going to be writing a story about the *Seahawk* for a New York newspaper.

"Just hope that doesn't bring a bunch of tourists here," one man responded.

"Now, I bet John here would disagree with you," Claire said. "Bet he'd like to see more customers at his place."

"More customers is good," John said, preparing to cook the hot dogs.

"I guess we want the place to be popular, but not too popular," the man added.

"Hey, David, over here," Tyler yelled, standing over an open cooler.

"Come on," Claire said, "do you want a beer or soda?"

"A beer sounds good."

"He'll take a beer," Claire said, as they joined Tyler.

"Hi, Tyler; thanks for inviting me to join you and Claire."

"Glad you could make it. Surprised you haven't attended one before," Tyler said, handing David a beer.

"Thanks."

"So, when did you get back into town?" Tyler asked.

"Got in Wednesday."

"Guess that house is keeping you busy."

"Yea, it sure is."

"Oh, I almost forgot," Tyler said, reaching into his breast pocket. "Here's your food ticket."

"Thanks, how much do I owe you?"

"You don't owe us a thing," Claire quickly responded.

"Thanks, guys, you're real hosts."

More and more people were showing up. Families

were spreading out blankets on the grass for their picnics. Assorted concession stands were selling food and merchandise. In an open grass area, a well-attended Frisbee game was in play, and off to the side, was a game of horseshoes taking place. The festivities were in full swing.

"I'll have to say it feels a bit odd being here," David said.

"Why's that?" Claire asked.

"I kind of feel like I am going back in time to Danny's story. He told me how they attended the first Blessing of the Fleet here."

"The first Blessing of the Fleet?" Tyler asked.

"That's what he said."

Claire, trying to imagine what it must have been like to hear this story, responded, "You should feel very honored he chose you to share that with."

"I don't know if the feeling is honored really. He probably picked me just because he knew I was a writer."

"So, how is the story coming along?" Tyler asked.

"I'm making progress, but one thing is bugging me about it—I don't know what part is missing."

"What d'ya mean, missing?"

"I can't help but wonder about the part of the story he didn't tell me. There's obviously more to it, but I'm afraid it went to the grave with him."

"Did you know that keepers of lights kept logs, just as they do on ships?" Claire asked.

"No, I wasn't aware of that," David responded. "That could be a great resource."

"That's what I was thinking," she said.

"Are those logs still around?"

"Not sure, but I don't see any problem with doing a little investigating," Claire said with a glow in her eyes.

This news gave David some hope. "When can we

do this?"

"Let's all plan on meeting at the lighthouse tomorrow after the Blessing of the Fleet. It's closed for the weekend, so it should be a good time."

"Sounds great. I'm psyched. Maybe my story has a chance after all," David said.

"Looks like they're serving up the grub. Let's get something to eat," Tyler said.

***

David was running late the next morning. When he entered the church, he found it was packed. As he looked around, he saw Claire waving to him and motioning him over. They had saved him a spot.

"Good morning," Claire said, as he slid into the pew next to her.

"Good morning."

Tyler, sitting on the other side of Claire leaned forward. "Morning."

David nodded back and then took a moment to look around the church.

"Is Helen here?" David whispered.

"No," Claire responded, "she hasn't attended a Blessing since Scott was lost. As you can imagine, it's difficult for her, and I don't mean just physically."

"I understand."

"Cynthia attends, though. She's over there." Claire nodded her head in the direction of the right front of the church.

David found himself revisiting Danny's story during the service. He had a new respect for the life of the fishermen, both past and present.

Afterward, they joined everyone in the churchyard where refreshments were being served by the young patrons, with some help from the Sunday school teachers.

"Hey, David, you wanna join Claire and me for brunch? We're meeting some friends over at Charley's diner."

"Sure, I could use something to eat."

David arrived shortly after Claire and Tyler. Pulling up to the diner, he found himself thinking about the past—the days when he would come here for lunch with his uncle. He sat in his car a moment, allowing the memories to surface. He had felt privileged to come here with his uncle, just the two of them. He would always order the same thing—a grilled cheese sandwich and what he called the clear Coke, which was really a Sprite. He was not allowed to drink sodas at home, but Uncle Walter let him.

The diner, a stainless steel rectangle structure, was built back in the early 1950s. It sat on a brick foundation and had red and blue neon lights that wrapped around all sides. David took a quick look around, as he walked through the door. In front of him was a counter that stretched the length of the restaurant, with stools fixed to the floor. Opposite the counter, with a narrow path between them, were booths; the booths lined the windows.

As David approached their table, Tyler remarked, "Geez, David, what route did you take? I thought you were right behind us."

"I must have taken the scenic route," David replied.

The diner was full this late morning, with only a few counter seats open. The short-order cook was busy at the grill, flipping hash browns and omelets while his assistant assembled fruit dishes. A young server with her hair pulled back tight in a ponytail made her rounds with the coffeepot, filling the white porcelain mugs, and then reaching into her apron for the packets of cream and placing two each at every mug filled.

"This is David Parker. He's Gina Murray's nephew. You know Kay; this is Chery, Sean, and Dawson," Tyler said, pointing around the table.

"Nice to meet you all," David said, nodding to them and taking a seat next to Chery.

"We're sorry to hear about your aunt," Chery said.

The server took everyone's order, as the group talked about the service and commented on how the altar looked decorated with all the fishing paraphernalia.

"I'm familiar with the *Seahawk*, but what about the other vessels they mentioned in the service. What are the stories behind their demise?" David asked.

"There was the fishing boat *My Lady*. She was lost in 1952," Dawson said.

"It was July 14," Claire broke in.

"She was grounded in a storm off the north side of Fishers Island. The whole crew was lost," Dawson went on. "Then, there was *The Echo II* in 1955." He paused and nodded at Claire, as she added, "January 12."

"She was on her way back in, when a storm hit. She went down off Cornfield Point. Luckily, though, three crewmen were rescued. They had quite a story to tell. There were six men aboard. The storm hit in the middle of the night. It wasn't that severe. As a matter of fact, one man was in his bunk, sleeping at the time. It was the angle of the wave. It came crashing down and split the boat in two. Before the men could react, they found themselves in the water. They didn't even have time to send out a distress call. The man who was sleeping was never found. The remaining men tried to stay together, but the waves kept separating them. When dawn arrived, only three men remained, clinging to debris. They were picked up by another fishing boat. All were in pretty bad shape."

"You say you're familiar with the Seahawk?" Dawson asked.

"Yes, I spoke to Danny Pierce about that incident. He talked to me about the captain, his brother-in-law, Scott."

"You spoke to Danny about this?" Sean broke in. "I didn't think he talked to anyone about that."

"I'm a writer. I think he wanted to finally tell his story," David answered, as their food arrived.

"When did you talk to him?" asked Dawson.

"I was talking to him in the days before his death."

"That's creepy," Kay commented.

"So, what's there to tell? It was lost in a storm; that makes for a pretty short story," Dawson asked.

"Scott had a family—a family with plans for the future," David replied.

"I suppose you're right," Dawson said. "I just figured since there weren't any witnesses to the sinking itself, it's kind of hard to describe."

Once everyone finished eating, Dawson jumped up from his seat. "So is anyone up for a parade?"

Everyone responded collectively, "Yes, we are."

"Then, let's get outta here."

Once in the parking lot, Tyler asked David, "Are you planning to watch the parade?"

"Actually, I was thinking about getting back to the house to finish up some things."

"No, that won't do," Claire responded. "You can't miss the parade nor can you miss the Blessing."

"There's no place to park," David said.

"You can park in that lot behind the library; it's not a far walk to Main Street."

David did not want to seem rude; they had been so accommodating. Besides, it sounded more interesting than getting the house stuff done.

75

"I guess I don't have any more excuses then. I'll meet you there."

The Stuart Cove residents and tourists had already assembled along Main Street. As the three of them joined the crowd, Claire yelled out, "Hurry up; follow me."

"You better listen to her," Tyler said.

They began running through the crowd.

"It's not easy keeping up with you," David yelled.

"I know the perfect vantage point," Claire called back.

They continued making their way through the crowd. Once they reached Claire's perfect spot, they watched the parade already in progress. There were the Knights of Columbus, the Port Evens Police Honor Guard, the American Legion Post #85, local sport teams, and the Stuart Cove Fire Department. There were floats of boats and seaside memorials; there were antique cars and pirates. They continued to watch as Stuart Cove celebrated the event.

"This might be a stupid question, but who is that?" David asked Claire.

"That's St. Andrew, the patron saint of fishermen," Claire responded, as a large decorated trailer carrying the statue passed by.

"Oh, yea, now I remember Danny telling me about that."

Suddenly, Claire shouted, "Come on; let's go," and she took off through the crowd.

"But it's not over," David yelled, as he and Tyler desperately tried to keep up with her.

"We have to get down to the docks."

They darted in and out of the crowd, soon arriving at the wharf where others were beginning to gather. Colorfully decorated fishing boats and a few leisure boats were lining up.

"I don't remember Danny telling me about all these decorations."

"They probably didn't do this back then," Claire said.

"Hey, you guys, see you made it," Kay said, as Chery, Sean, and Dawson joined her.

It wasn't long before a large crowd appeared, led by Father Kealy.

"I told you this was a good spot," Claire shouted over the noise of the crowd.

"I guess that's why you're the tour guide."

Claire smiled back.

Father Kealy, accompanied by clergymen of nearby churches, proceeded to the end of the pier where he took his place at the podium.

Tapping on the microphone, he asked, "Can everyone hear me?"

A loud YES was the response from the crowd.

"Before we proceed with the Blessing, I would like everyone to join me in prayer:

> Holy Father, you have given the seas and the life they contain for the use and benefit of all. Protect our fishermen during this fishing season and give them a bountiful catch. May God in Heaven fulfill abundantly the prayers which are pronounced over you and your boats on the occasion of the Blessing of the Fleet. God bless your going out and coming in;

The Lord be with you at
home and on the water.
Amen.

The crowd responded, "Amen." Father Kealy then left the podium. As each boat passed, he sprinkled holy water and gave his blessing.

"Are you enjoying this, David?" Claire asked.

"I sure am."

"After the boats receive their blessing, they go out farther and form a circle, then one of the boats throws a wreath out onto the water, in memory of our deceased fishermen," Claire explained.

"Like Scott Spear?"

"Yes, like Scott Spear."

***

They had agreed to meet at the lighthouse that evening, but when David drove up to the keeper's house, he only saw Claire.

"Where's Tyler?" David asked, getting out of his car.

"He decided to skip it. This just isn't his *cup of tea*, so to speak," Claire said, as they approached the front door together. Not wanting to address Tyler's absence further, she went on, "Now, I'll have you know I have permission from Mr. Baker, the president of the historical society to do this, so I'm not breaking in," Claire explained, unlocking the door to the keeper's house.

With a slight chuckle, David responded, "I wasn't accusing you of anything."

As they entered the front hallway, Claire quickly went into the gift shop.

"Just a moment, I have to turn off the alarm."

"I didn't think you had to lock your doors around

78

here, much less have an alarm system."

"Afraid this place has had its share of break-ins over the years. Odd thing is they don't seem to take anything, or even disturb anything, just break in. The alarm was finally installed; didn't have a problem after that."

David walked into the living room, soon followed by Claire. Pointing at the *Master of the Seas* painting, he asked, "You remember telling me about that picture?"

"Yes."

"That was supposed to be a housewarming gift from Danny to Helen and Scott."

With an inquisitive look on her face, Claire responded, "Danny told you that?"

"Yes, he did."

"Where did Danny get it?"

"He got it from a local antique dealer. Apparently, the dealer didn't know what he had, so Danny got a real bargain. Didn't Danny talk to anyone about his time here as the last keeper?"

"No, as I said before, he couldn't, as a matter of fact, he didn't talk much to anyone about anything. He turned into a real loner—very reclusive."

"That's a pity, 'cause I bet the historical society could have benefited from the information he had."

They walked around through the foyer and into the hallway. "We have a photograph of Danny and his family taken by the Coast Guard." Claire pointed to one of the black-and-white photographs hanging on the wall. There, looking back at David was Danny, Scott, Helen, and Cynthia in Helen's arms. They were standing together in front of the lighthouse. "I'll be right back," Claire said, leaving David there to examine the picture.

As he looked into the faces, David was overtaken by an odd feeling—Danny's story was there in front of him, seeming as if it had come to life.

Hearing Claire coming back down the stairs, David turned to find her carrying a large box.

"Let me help you with that."

"Thanks. A lot of the records are in the lighthouse office, but I thought this box might have some interesting paperwork as well."

They continued through the hallway and out the backdoor.

"You're not scared of heights, are you?" Claire turned and asked. "You've been to the gallery, right?"

"Yes, Claire. Don't you remember Jim took me on a tour?"

"Just wanna make sure. Lots of people can't do those stairs," Claire said, unlocking the door of the lighthouse. "Now, be careful taking that box up, take it slow."

They wound their way up to the office area where David set the box down on top of a table in the room. Claire retrieved two more boxes tucked away in a corner.

"I've been meaning to do this ever since I started working here."

They began removing the paperwork from each box and sorting it in date order.

"Gosh, I hope you didn't have any plans tonight; looks like this might take a while," David said.

"That's fine. I actually enjoy this; it's uncovering history."

"What made you so interested in this stuff?" David asked.

Continuing to rummage through the paperwork, Claire replied, "My father used to work for the Coast Guard; part of his job was visiting the area lighthouses, checking up on them. He told me stories about his visits; I was fascinated. He used to read me a bedtime story called *The Lighthouse Keeper* when I was a little girl. It was about a family living in a lighthouse—a mother, father, and two children, a young boy and a girl who was my age at the time. They had a cat named Thomas, a cow name Betsy, and some chickens. The lighthouse was on a small island out at sea. It was only them on this island, so the kids had to find things to do to entertain themselves. They had many adventures there on the island. I loved that story, and I especially loved it when he would read it to me. Ever since, I have had a special place in my heart for lighthouses and related nautical history.

"Where is your father now?" David asked.

Claire looked down and replied, "I'm afraid he passed away a few years ago."

"I'm sorry," David replied. "Is your mother still around?

"Yes, but she moved to Florida after dad died. She loves it, but I don't get to see her as much as I'd like to. How about you?"

"I lost my mother, but my father's still around. He still lives in Philadelphia. I visit him when I can."

They turned their attention back to their task.

"There's some old stuff here. Look at this," David said, handing Claire a faded piece of paper.

"1934, that's from the days before the Coast Guard. It was the U.S. Lighthouse Service back then."

They continued their quest into the night, pouring over the paperwork. They found supply orders, letters, even a couple old copies of the booklet *Instructions to Light-Keepers*.

"I found the logs," Claire yelled, barely able to hold back her excitement. "Before we dig in, you thirsty? We've been at this for a while now. There should be some sodas in the house. How about I get us a couple?"

"Nothing stronger than a soda, like maybe a beer?"

"'Fraid not. Promise me you won't peak inside those logs until I get back."

"Okay, I promise."

As soon as Claire left, David got up to stretch his legs. He realized once she left the room that he felt a little relieved. He found himself attracted to Claire and was enjoying the time he was spending with her. As he paced the room, he tried to reason with himself. *What the hell are you thinking? She has a boyfriend, and you live in New York. Get a hold of yourself.* Oddly, David began to feel a slight chill in the air, causing him to abandon his thoughts of Claire and instead attempt to figure out the source of the cold air. Then, suddenly, David thought he heard a sound. He turned around and looked in the direction it came from.

"What the hell!" David said aloud, as his attention was directed at the channel receiver.

There was no mistaking it. The radio was coming on, first relaying static. David quickly moved in close to listen.

"Mayday—mayday—mayday—mayday—
mayday—mayday, this is the fishing vessel *Seahawk*, our coordinates ...."

The alert was then interrupted with more static.

"... we are taking on water ..." More static. "... need help."

Then nothing, the radio went quiet.

"I'm back with food and drink," Claire announced, entering the room from the staircase.

David was standing in front of the radio; his face was pale.

"What's wrong? You look like you've seen a ghost," Claire said, quickly putting down the basket of refreshments.

"I have."

"What? What d'ya mean?"

"What's today's date?" David asked, still in shock.

"It's August 1st," Claire replied.

"You're not going to believe this. That radio just came on, and I heard a mayday call from the *Seahawk*." As David said this, he fell into the nearest chair.

Claire walked over to the radio, looked behind it, reached back, and with the end of the power cord in her hand, said, "It couldn't have; it's not even plugged in. Not only that, it hasn't worked in years. We've tried it."

"Claire, I know this sounds crazy, but I know what I heard."

Claire stared at David. She wanted to believe him, but how could she?

"The logs, we have to check the logs," David said in a panic.

Each grabbed a book and scanned the dates, then tossed it aside and moved to the next book until Claire announced, "I have it—1956."

She rapidly turned the pages until she approached July, then *August 1, 1956*. She read aloud, "*A catastrophe has occurred at Stone Ridge Lighthouse. A mayday call came in from the* Seahawk *at 10:05 p.m. during the storm Dale. I had no light to bring them home. Danny Pierce.*"

Claire paused, "Oh, my God, what's this?"

"What?" David said, looking over her shoulder.

"There's more here. '*August 1, 1957, I come back here because being around Helen is too difficult. I think I'm going crazy because I just heard the* Seahawk *mayday call again. They turned my light off. Danny Pierce.*'"

"Oh, my God," David said, his face again turning pale. "Do you believe me now?"

"Yes, I think I do."

They continued to read the log. There was a similar

83

entry for 1965.

"It looks as if he came back again in 1972, but he didn't make note of the distress call," Claire noted.

"So, maybe it didn't happen then."

"I expect if it did, he would have written it down. Keepers are usually very particular about what they put in their logs." Claire continued reading, "Looks like he returns sporadically over the years. Sometimes, he hears it, and sometimes, he doesn't. The last entry is 1995." She pauses. "That's when the alarm system was installed; he must have stopped coming here after that."

They both looked at each other, trying to absorb it all.   After a few moments of silence, David quietly said, "So, Danny, does this tell the whole story?"

They decided to keep the experience and the information in the logs to themselves until they could figure out how best to deal with it. David, being in the reporting and writing business realized it was a delicate situation and must be handled carefully. That took some convincing because Claire was visibly upset. They packed up the boxes and put them in a safe place.

As they made their way back inside the keeper's house, David asked, "You're probably going to want to tell Tyler about this, aren't you?"

"NO, I don't," Claire quickly responded. "I really don't want to talk to anyone about it. Frankly I feel a little weird about the whole thing. At this point, I just want to go home."

She reset the alarm, and they went to their cars. David was still shook up by what had happened, but he was also concerned about Claire and its effect on her.

"Are you going to be okay, Claire?" he asked.

"I'm fine, just want to put this behind me right now and get some rest."

David, keeping his distance so she would not

notice, followed her home. He wanted to make sure she got there okay. He noticed she turned onto a dead-end road. He slowed down and saw what he suspected was her house, so he drove on home.

***

David woke up in a start, as the events of the night before quickly emerged into his consciousness. It seemed as incredible in the morning light as it did in the dark of the night. He lay there going over the course of events in his mind: Danny's story, the logs, and the radio—especially the radio. David had always put himself in the category of a skeptic when it came to the paranormal, but this experience changed everything. He was not comfortable with that.

He decided the best thing to do was to get busy and hopefully get distracted from his thoughts. It was at that moment, the phone rang.

"Hello."

"David, this is Claire."

He was glad to hear her voice, but did not want to make that apparent.

"Hi, Claire, how are you doing today? Better than last night?"

"I'm not doing that great. I'm at work right now, and I'm having a hard time concentrating. Was that a dream, or did what happen last night really happen?"

"I'm afraid it did. Have you talked to anyone about it?"

"No, I haven't; you're the only one I can talk to about it. If anyone else told me this story, I would have thought they were nuts."

"You're right, maybe the best thing to do is to try and forget about it."

"That's not easy, David."

"I know, but you'll make yourself nuts thinking about it."

"Yea, I guess you're right. When are you going back to New York?"

"A week from today."

"Are you still going to write your story about the *Seahawk*?"

"I'm going to have to think about it."

"Might get people's attention," Claire remarked.

"Yea, and I can image what will happen to my reputation."

"I guess I should be getting back to work. We'll see you before you leave?"

"I'd like that. See ya, Claire."

Soon after she hung up the phone, Tyler walked into the office.

"You want to go to lunch?"

"No, thanks, I'm not real hungry."

"How did it go last night with the research?"

Claire hesitated, and he noticed she was feeling uncomfortable.

"What's wrong? What happened last night?"

"Nothing special, just looked through old paperwork," Claire responded, trying to conceal her uneasiness.

"I know you; there's something you're not telling me."

Claire knew he was right on both accounts. She and Tyler had been together for almost two years. During that time, their relationship had become serious, serious enough that he had asked her to marry him. It took some convincing on her part for him to agree to leave the arrangement status quo until she finished school. Claire was comfortable in the relationship, though, aside from the fact that he did not understand her interest in nautical history and sometimes resented the fact she spent time at the lighthouse.

"Tyler, it's nothing. I'm just not feeling well today."

He was not satisfied with her response, but felt he was not going to convince her to explain her obvious discomfort—not yet, anyway.

***

David stuck to his personal promise and kept himself busy, working on the house and his novel. As a result, his last week was turning out to be very productive. Every time the events of that evening entered his thoughts, he was able to bury them with a writing technique he had perfected. He liked to call this technique "forget it." After he finished the draft of a story, he would put it in the back of his mind and forget it, then come back to it later for a rewrite. He found himself trying to use that same method when he began thinking about Claire, but in that case, he was not very successful.

With the auction scheduled for that afternoon, David had to get some last minute jobs done. He was cutting the grass when he felt his cell phone go off.

"Hi, David, it's Claire. How would you like to join Tyler and me later. We're going to meet up with some friends for lunch at Riverside."

"Actually, that sounds great. That gives me an excuse not to be here for the auction. What time?"

"We'll meet you there at half past twelve," Claire said, as Tyler came into the room shaking his head.

"See you then."

"Bye."

"Did you just invite David?"

"Yes, I did. Is there a problem with that?"

"I guess not, but it would have been nice if you asked me first," Tyler replied, obviously bothered by it."

"I didn't think you'd mind. He's going back to New York in a couple of days; thought we'd say good-bye."

"That's fine, Claire. Have you seen my sunglasses?"

"No."

Tyler's reaction surprised Claire. Jealousy was not an emotion he had exhibited before. She watched him, clearly annoyed, looking for his sunglasses. She felt this meant Tyler did not trust her. This thought saddened her, but it quickly turned to anger. Why didn't Tyler trust her? What had she done to warrant that reaction? Before she could address this with him, Tyler called out, "I'll be right back, I have to run to the store for a minute."

"What store?" she called back to him, but he was already out the door.

They were not a couple who fought about things, and Claire wanted to keep it that way, so she decided to talk to Tyler about it on their way to lunch. It turned out she wouldn't have the chance, though. Tyler called some time later to tell her that he got held up running errands and would instead meet her there.

"I thought you were just going to the store for a minute," Claire said to him when he called.

"That was the plan, but then I saw that the drills finally went on sale, and my plan changed."

"So, did you get one?"

"Yes, I did—got a good deal too."

He seemed to be in a better mood, so rather than risk changing that, she decided not to bring up the earlier conversation.

"I'll be there in about thirty minutes," she said and hung up the phone.

***

After taking a quick walk around the inside of the restaurant, David figured the group must have grabbed a table outside. The riverside restaurant had outside dining on the surrounding dock. It had turned out to be a hot day, but with the slight breeze off the water and under the protection of the large umbrellas, it was bearable.

"David, glad you could meet us," Claire said, as he joined them at the table.

"You remember Kay, Chery, Sean, and this is Larry."

"Hello," David said to everyone, as he reached out to shake Larry's hand."

"How 'ya been?" Kay asked.

"Been real busy working on the house—almost done, though."

"When are you going back to New York?" Sean asked.

"I'm headed back on Monday."

The server approached the table and asked David if he wanted something to drink.

"I'll take a Sam Adams, thanks."

"So, they're doing the auction today?" Claire asked.

"Yea, hopefully, they'll sell everything, but whatever they don't sell, they'll donate."

"So, you'll be going back to an empty house then," Claire added.

"That's right; I plan on staying at a hotel the next couple of nights, while I finish up my aunt's affairs."

"You have a buyer yet?" Tyler asked.

"No, expect that might take a little time."

"So, how's that story about the *Seahawk* coming along," Chery asked.

"Kind of on hold right now," David answered, as the server brought him his beer.

"You writing a story about the *Seahawk*?" Larry asked.

"I might."

"What's there to write? It was lost during tropical storm Dale," Larry added.

"I had a talk with Danny about it before he passed. He shared a lot of information with me."

"I know everyone liked Danny. They kind of felt sorry for him and what happened, but wasn't he a bit of a kook? The way I hear it, he spent most of his life out fishing while he was actually looking for the *Seahawk*. Now, if that isn't crazy, I don't know what is," Larry continued.

Hearing this angered David, even though this was David's assessment during the time he spent with Danny. It was after he learned the whole story that his opinion changed. He began to understand Danny and what he was going through. As he felt the urge to defend Danny, it became apparent to David that he felt a sense of loyalty. It was at that moment that he decided he *would* write the story.

"I think you have him all wrong," David responded.

"Me and half the town."

David felt his cell phone go off. He checked to see who was calling. As he answered, he excused himself from the table and went to a quiet corner.

"Hi, Ellen."

"Hi, David, I hope I'm not disturbing you, but I need to talk to you about the house."

"What's up?" David asked.

"I was approached by a couple who would very much like to rent it."

"Rent? I thought we agreed it was to be sold."

"Yes, you're right, but this couple heard about it going on the market. They can't afford to buy it right now, but they're ready to move in and rent it. I thought I'd run it by you."

"I'll have to think about this, Ellen. Clearly this changes things. How about I give you a call later?"

"That's fine, David. You think about it, and I'll wait to hear from you."

David's first impulse was to reject this idea, but rather than make a snap decision, he told himself to think about it.

"Sorry about that," David said, as he rejoined everyone at the table.

"So, are you going to give us a hint of what's going to be in the story you might write?" Larry asked.

"I can't give that away. You'll have to wait and see," David responded.

The conversation visibly unnerved Claire, which did not go unnoticed by Tyler. She decided to try to change the subject.

"So, what's it like living in New York?" she asked.

David, too, was aware of Claire's uneasiness, and he also knew what she was trying to do.

"It's very different," David replied, as the server returned to take everyone's order.

***

Claire met up with Tyler at his place later that evening for dinner. Afterward, they took the bottle of wine out on the deck.

"I need you to be honest with me," Tyler said with sternness in his voice.

"What d'ya mean? Honest about what?" Claire responded, knowing where this was going.

"Something happened that night when you were with David at the lighthouse, and I need you to tell me what that was."

"What do you think happened?" she asked, again angered by his mistrust.

"I don't know; you tell me."

"Do you think I had some fling with David that night?"

"Claire, I don't know what the hell to think, but something happened. You're not hiding it very well."

Claire did not want to talk about it. She had made a promise to David. Besides, the whole incident made her feel uneasy. She had to agree that she had not done a very good job of hiding her reaction to the events. She began to wonder how she would feel if the tables were turned and it was he that seemed to be hiding something.

"Something did happen, but it wasn't a fling," she finally admitted.

"Did he make a pass at you?"

"No, it was nothing like that," Claire said, irritated by the questions.

"Claire, we must trust each other. You need to be open with me."

"Trust each other?" Claire shouted. "You didn't trust me. You think I jumped in the sack with David; how is that trust?"

"Okay, we're both guilty, but if something is bothering you, you have to tell me what it is."

Claire realized he was right. How could she keep this from him?

She paused for a while, and Tyler patiently allowed her to collect her thoughts. Then, she began to recount the events, "We were in the lighthouse office going through old paperwork for a while, so I figured it was time for a break and went into the house to get a couple of sodas.

When I returned to the office, I noticed David was shaken up by something."

"What happened?" Tyler asked.

"He said that a distress call from the *Seahawk* had just come across the radio, which by the way, was not plugged in, much less in working order."

"WHAT?" Tyler responded, totally mystified.

"He was very upset," Claire continued. "Then, we began looking through the logs and found the date the *Seahawk* was lost." She paused. "We found an entry written by Danny exactly a year later, where he noted a mayday call. There were more entries on that date, sporadically through the years, same thing—a mayday call from the *Seahawk*."

Tyler sat back in his chair and began to laugh.

"You've got to be kidding me. Don't you see, Claire? David has played you for a fool. He must have found those entries in the log while you were out of the room, and then figured he'd claim it happened to him too. He's a writer; he wants his articles to sell papers. You're the perfect witness, even though you weren't actually there."

Claire was irritated by Tyler's assumption that David was lying and for implying that she was naive.

"Think about it, Claire. It doesn't pass the smell test; it's crazy."

"What about the logs?" she asked, trying to defend her position.

"You said they were written by Danny. Hasn't his emotional state already been established? He could have written that, but it doesn't mean it actually happened."

Claire again paused, thinking about that evening. *Could Tyler be right?* She began to question her judgment.

"Shit, Claire, all this worry about that—you really had me going," Tyler said, laughing as he took the bottle of wine and went back into the house.

**

A strange sensation came over David, as he walked into the empty house. Standing in the middle of the living room, he looked into the empty rooms. He tried to come to terms with this response by reasoning with himself. Wasn't this my goal—to get it ready to sell, to move on? He remembered the day when Ellen first called about selling the house. It seemed a long time ago, even though it had only been a month. He thought about how he had felt when the daunting task of getting the place ready was in front of him. Now, with it done, he had to face the fact that his periodic visits to Stuart Cove were probably ending. He continued to walk through each room, remembering events occurring throughout the years. The most difficult was the porch, the place where the rocking chairs once were, now void. Making his way out into the backyard, looking out over the water, he remembered what Danny had told him. *Everything happens for a reason.* Taking his cell phone from his pocket, he called Ellen.

"Hello, Stuart Cove Reality. Ellen speaking. Can I help you?"

"Ellen, it's David. Is that couple still interested in renting my place?"

"Yes, they keep calling me, asking if I heard back from you."

"Well, you can tell them I am interested in renting to them."

Chapter Seven

"You know you don't have to leave. You did me a favor staying here while I was in Stuart Cove," David said, grabbing a couple of beers from the kitchen.

"I don't want to wear out my welcome. Besides, it's time I start bothering Paul," Lance said, as David handed him a beer.

"You can do what you like, but it's not a problem if you want to stay here. I'll kick you out when you become too much of a pain in the ass."

"Thanks, buddy, but Paul's expecting me. Wouldn't want to deprive him of the opportunity to room with such a cool guy as myself."

"Yeh, I guess there is that," David responded, smiling to himself.

"I'm going to find a place real soon. though. I can feel it in my bones," Lance said, finishing his beer.

"If you quit being so damn picky, maybe you will."

Lance got up and headed for the kitchen, "You want another beer?"

"Can't, I've got a press conference I have to attend tonight."

"Who the hell has a press conference at night?"

"I guess someone who doesn't really want one," David answered, unhappy with the fact he had to go back to work.

David was finding it difficult to adjust to his life back in New York; his sense of stress was more noticeable. Situations he used to blow off were affecting his outlook. Unlike his previous return from Stuart Cove, this time, he did not know when, or if, he would be going back there.

David began gathering information for Danny's

story. He was uncomfortable with the idea, but he realized that he would have to start with the paranormal mayday call he witnessed. Recognizing this could bring back the fear and despair he had felt that night, David struggled with the notion. What had happened to him affected his viewpoint on life itself, and the thought of possibly talking to someone besides Claire about it was extremely troubling. David went to the library and found a limited number of books on the subject. Scanning one of these, he found a local paranormal investigator, and he was able to find the investigator's Web site. Then, when he felt he could not delay the decision further, David e-mailed him.

***

"This is Owen Skinner, the paranormal investigator you e-mailed. Did I call you at a bad time?"

"Owen, thanks for calling. No, it's not a bad time," David replied.

"I'm interested in talking to you about your experience, Do you have time to meet this Wednesday evening, say around seven o'clock?"

"Sure, I think I can pull that off, but in case I have to work late, I'll give you a call. My schedule can be pretty crazy."

Owen's experience as an investigator taught him that the best place to interview a witness was either at the site of the event or a place where they felt most comfortable. He acknowledged the fact that witnesses did not always relay their stories freely, that it could be a very difficult experience to relive in an interview. Owen prided himself on his professionalism and the care he showed toward his clients, even though he did not charge for his services.

After getting David's address, Owen tried to assure him that he was doing the right thing by contacting an investigator.

As the evening of the interview approached, David felt a desire to call and cancel. During these occasions, he had to remind himself that he was doing the right thing. It was a necessary step in the process of dealing with the experience and ultimately telling Danny's story.

"Owen, come in, glad you could meet with me," David said, leading Owen into the living room.

"I was very intrigued by your story."

"If it hadn't happened to me, I would have never believed it," David replied, motioning Owen to sit in the chair across from the couch. "Can I get you something to drink?"

"No, thank you, I'm fine."

David had already poured himself a glass of wine, hoping to take the edge off his anxiety.

"Do you mind if I record our conversation?" Owen asked. "I find this to be more efficient than taking notes."

"No, I guess not."

Owen gave off an emanation that caused David to immediately feel comfortable. Few people possess this trait. It is not something you can learn; you have it, or you don't. And Owen had it, which worked well in his line of work. As Owen retrieved his recorder from his pants pocket, David closely observed him. He appeared to be slightly older than David, which David guessed put him in his early thirties. He had a thin face with a goatee that was mostly dark but included a hint of gray. David chuckled to himself at the thought of those gray hairs possibly appearing after a scary experience he might have had. He wore jeans and a tee shirt that displayed *I'd Rather Be Ghost Hunting* across its chest. David relaxed, knowing this person was interested in his experience, and he would not judge David adversely for the encounter he witnessed. Owen placed the recorder on the coffee table sitting between them.

"So, this occurred in Connecticut?" Owen asked.

"Yes, I was there to settle my aunt's affairs after she passed away. It started when I was approached by an old man who felt compelled to tell me a story about his past as a lighthouse keeper and the events surrounding the loss of the fishing vessel *Seahawk* during a bad storm. His sister, her husband, and their baby girl lived with him at the lighthouse. Her husband was lost at sea.

Owen listened intensely. It was his policy to allow the client to complete the story, not to interrupt, and not to ask any questions until he felt the moment was right.

"They were about to close down the lighthouse. They had already turned off the light and replaced it with another beacon located at Black Sand State Park. The guy, Danny, died before he finished telling me his story."

This news sparked Owen's interest. He nodded, as David continued.

"Danny, as he put it, 'had a story to tell.' He knew I was a writer, so I guess that's why he came to me." Still troubled by this thought, David paused. "After his death, I decided I would write his story. At that time, I thought I might start off with an article in the *Daily Post*, where I work, but now it's turning out to be bigger than that. Claire, a woman I met, who gives tours of the Stone Ridge Lighthouse, was helping me with research for the story, and she arranged for us to go through records there at the lighthouse one night. I didn't realize at the time, but we were there on the anniversary of the accident. At exactly 10:05 that night, the radio transmitter in the lighthouse's office suddenly turned on, and I heard a mayday call from the *Seahawk*. The damn thing wasn't even turned on or plugged in. Let me tell you, nothing like that has ever happened to me before, and I'm kind of sorry it did." David paused. "I feel as if I'm carrying this burden, that there's something else Danny wanted from me. Anyway, we then rifled through the lighthouse logs and found that Danny had been coming back to the lighthouse, breaking in actually, every few years on the anniversary and experiencing the same mayday call. Sure I can't get you some wine?" David asked, pouring himself another glass.

"No, thanks," Owen replied, allowing David time to absorb the story he had just exposed. Sensing it was now the right time for questions, Owen asked, "Did Claire witness the mayday call?"

"No, she had left the room to get us something to drink," David replied.

"That's okay; I just find it helpful to talk to everyone who witnessed the event, if possible. Did you notice anything unusual right before the call—a smell, a change in temperature?"

Thinking back to the event, David replied, "I noticed the area becoming cold right beforehand. I thought Claire had turned up the air. No odd smell, though."

"Were there reports of any other activity? Is the place known for being haunted?"

"No, not that I'm aware of. Claire didn't mention that." Then, David stopped. "Well, there was one thing. The guy who gave me the tour of the lighthouse mentioned the radio was haunted. Don't know where that came from, though."

"Have you had any experiences here in New York?" Owen asked.

"No, not before, nor since, that night, thank goodness."

"What time did you say the mayday call came in?"

"It was at 10:05, same as the time listed in the log."

"So, Danny didn't talk to you about the mayday call?"

"No, he told me about the night of the storm when the *Seahawk* was lost. We had planned to meet the following day, but he died that night. Something he said stays with me. He would say, 'Everything happens for a reason.'"

"I think he's right," Owen replied.

"So, what does this all mean? How can I get rid of this burden I feel?" David asked, now putting his full trust in this person who was just recently a stranger to him.

Owen leaned forward and with poise explained, "What you experienced is known as a psychic recording or a residual haunting. This is considered non-intelligent—the ghost, or entity, is an energy that is somehow trapped. It replays itself, like replaying a recording. You will usually see this in a case where an apparition walks a particular path repeatedly. It might be weekly, or it might be yearly. It might be replaying an act it did repeatedly in life. In cases where a ghost has been seen walking through a wall of a house, it is revealed many times, on further research, that the wall was once a door. Now, this is the first time I have heard of a device being used to replay the recording."

David listened to this explanation with intense concentration.

Owen continued, "I expect the mayday call was the last act before his demise. Some say the dead don't realize they died."

"That's disturbing," David responded. "Does that mean they might be stuck between this life and whatever is beyond?"

"I don't know what your religious beliefs are, but

this is where it gets complicated and personal," Owen replied. "You said that when the storm hit, the light was already extinguished?"

"Yes," David replied.

"Did Danny mention this when he talked to you about it?"

"Yes, he did. He obviously felt guilty and responsible for what happened. That was a burden he carried for the rest of his life. Now, I feel as if he's passed that on to me," David replied, obviously moved by this revelation.

"I might have a solution for you," Owen said.

Hearing this, David moved to the edge of the sofa and leaned in toward Owen, "I'm all ears; what's the solution?"

"You need to turn the light back on. It needs to be on for the next anniversary."

David thought about this for a moment, "How the hell am I going to do that?"

"I know a local guy through my work investigating lighthouses who's involved in lighthouse restorations. I'm sure he has his connections. Maybe he knows of someone in Connecticut we can contact who can look at your light and see what it'll take."

"I guess there's no harm in that, but I'd be pretty damn surprised if that's even a possibility," David said, finally taking notice of the wine glass in front of him on the coffee table.

"Of course, I can't guarantee this will solve your dilemma, but everything seems to point in that direction," Owen said matter-of-factly.

"In an odd way, what you say seems to make sense," David replied.

"Do you have any other questions for me?" Owen asked, his concern and inquiry genuine.

David thought for a moment, "No, I think you've addressed everything."

"You have my number. Please call me if you think of anything else—any questions or if you need to talk to someone about it. I'll get a hold of the lighthouse guy and let you know what I find out."

"Thanks, Owen, you've been very helpful. It's nice to know that Danny and I aren't crazy and that others have experienced weird stuff like this."

"You'd be surprised how many people have, from all backgrounds and positions," Owen replied, getting up to leave.

As they reached the door, David reached out to shake his hand. "Thanks again, Owen, you have no idea how much this helps."

"Remember, call me if you need to."

After closing the door, David went back into the living room to gather the bottle of wine and his glass. As he walked into the kitchen, he thought about the conversation that had just taken place. Relief and purpose replaced the anxiety he initially felt. He now had to figure out how to get that light back on.

***

"Looks like I finally found a place," Lance said, storming through David's front door.

"That's good," David replied, hardly acknowledging his entrance.

"What's up with you?" Lance asked.

"I just had a weird phone call with Claire." Not wanting to reveal that he had called her to tell her about the meeting with the paranormal investigator, he instead said, "I called to see if I could talk to her about the history of the lighthouse."

"Yea, and what did she say to that?"

"She kind of blew me off; said she was really busy with schoolwork right now and probably wouldn't have time."

"So, maybe she doesn't. What's so weird about that?"

"It's not like I know her real well, but what I do know is that she is passionate about nautical history, and I don't think she'd pass up a chance to be part of this."

"It's her boyfriend," Lance replied.

"Tyler?"

"Yea, chances are he's getting jealous and probably told her to back off."

"I guess you could be right. I didn't take her for someone that would bow to his wishes, though, not when it had to do with lighthouses."

"Hey, you know you're interested in her. I'm sure he sensed that and probably made her feel bad about it. You know how that works. You're out of luck, man, unless you want to bust things up."

"I don't want to do that," David said, obviously torn by the thought.

Attempting to make light of the situation, David said, "So, tell me about the place you found—good price, good location?"

Lance went on to tell David all about the condo he saw that morning with his realtor. As David listened, he caught himself thinking back to the conversation with Claire. He realized he would have to come to terms with her wishes. That would be difficult enough, but there was also the lighthouse, how would he get it lit without her help?

***

"Don't say no."

"Lance, what d'ya want? I just got home," David said, balancing the phone up against his ear as he attempted to unlock his door with his briefcase in his other hand.

"You gotta promise me you're not gunna say no."

"I'm not promising a thing, and quit playing games. What the hell do you want?"

"I got us dates for Saturday night," Lance said.

"Did you? Why does that scare me?" David replied, finally getting into his apartment.

"Yea, Jennifer finally agreed to go out with me."

"I'm happy for you," David commented with sarcasm in his voice.

"And she has a friend who has no plans for Saturday, just like you."

"What a coincidence."

"Hey, Claire's out of the picture now."

"She was never in the picture, you ass," David replied, knowing this was the truth, but also saddened by the thought.

"So, is that a yes?" Lance asked.

After pausing for a moment, David replied, "It's a maybe. What did you have planned?"

"I thought we'd go to that murder mystery dinner theater," Lance replied.

"I've actually wanted to check that place out," David responded.

"Great, I'll let them know we're on."

As soon as David hung up the phone, he regretted his decision, but rather than call Lance back to cancel, he chose to go ahead with the plans. He found he had to justify this decision to himself, though. *I'm back working long hours. I've been consumed with Danny's story, and most of all, I need a distraction from Claire, a woman I have no business thinking about.*

***

"Where are you going?" Claire asked, as Tyler turned down Oak Street.

"I thought we'd go out to dinner at Mason's tonight."

"I have class."

"You can skip class tonight; we have better things to do," Tyler said, continuing to the restaurant.

"Tyler, you know I don't like skipping class. It just causes me more work. Why can't we go tomorrow night?"

"Because I have reservations for tonight."

"Is that why you wanted to drive me to work today, so you could kidnap me afterward?" she asked.

"You are one smart cookie," Tyler said with a laugh.

Claire was not pleased with Tyler's scheme and his disregard for her class. This thoughtless and egocentric behavior was a side of him that was becoming more apparent to Claire.

"I can't enjoy dinner if I'm thinking about all the work I have to catch up on.

"It'll be fine; stop worrying about it," Tyler said.

The sun was beginning to set this late September evening, as they pulled into the parking lot. When she got out of the car, Claire noticed the drop in temperature, so she reached into the backseat and grabbed her jacket. The restaurant, a brick structure occupying this quiet secluded location on King's Creek for more than forty years, had become a favorite for Claire and Tyler—the place they

105

came to celebrate different occasions or when they felt like going someplace a little bit special. Claire began to question Tyler's motives. It was not anyone's birthday; it was not their first date anniversary. She hoped he would not try to propose to her again, doubting that would be the case since she had made it quite clear that decision would be held off until after she finished school.

They walked up the steps to the front porch stretching the width of the structure. To the right of the front door, in large white rocking chairs, sat an elderly couple, each slowly rocking back and forth in rhythm with each other.

"Is there a wait for dinner?" Tyler asked.

"Oh, no," the gentleman answered, "we're just waiting for a friend and enjoying the evening."

Claire and Tyler entered the foyer and approached the young hostess standing behind the podium.

"Crofford," Tyler announced.

She looked down at her list to check the name. "This way, please," she said, taking two menus from the shelf in the podium.

They were led to a table near a large bay window. They took their seats, as the hostess handed them the menus. Claire looked out the window at Kings Creek, where two sailboats were motoring in for the evening, trying to outrun the setting sun.

"Can I start you off with something to drink?" the waiter asked, approaching the table.

"I'll take a Coors. How about you, dear?" Tyler asked.

"I'll take your house Merlot, please," Claire replied.

"It's a nice evening, isn't it?" Tyler asked, looking out the window.

A moment later, the waiter returned with their drinks.

"So, you're wondering why I dragged you out to dinner on a class night?"

"Yes, I am," Claire responded, sipping her wine.

"I have important news."

"You do, and what is this important news?"

"I was keeping it a secret because I didn't want to disappoint you if I didn't get it," Tyler said.

"Get what?"

"I got that position in Maine, and it comes with a hefty promotion."

"I had no idea you applied for that job," Claire responded, astonished at this revelation.

"I figure with this promotion, we can buy a place and you can go to school full-time. You don't have that much more to go, anyway."

Claire, struggling with what she was hearing, "What makes you think I want to leave Stuart Cove?"

Tyler paused, not expecting this reaction. "You said you liked Maine."

"Maybe to visit, but I haven't said anything about wanting to move there."

"You've been here all your life. You need to get out of your own backyard, Claire."

"I'm happy here, Tyler," she said, as the waiter returned to take their order.

"What can I get for you two?" the waiter asked.

"We're not ready yet," Tyler snapped back.

***

An odd melody sounded in David's dream. The sound continued for a moment, then, slowly waking up, he realized it was his phone, and not a dream.

"Hello," he said, not bothering to check the number.

"David, it's Claire."

107

The adrenalin suddenly running through his veins yanked him out of his sleepy haze. He looked over to see Tracey sleeping in his bed next to him, as the events of the night before registered in his mind.

Everyone met up at the dinner theater. David was the last to arrive, because he had trouble getting a taxi. As he approached the group in the lobby, he noticed Lance had his arm around one of the women. *This must be Jennifer*, David thought. The other woman was tall and had long black hair with bangs right above her eyebrows. She wore a short black dress clinging to her well-proportioned body. She was very attractive, which surprised David. She did not appear to be someone who would agree to go out on a blind date.

"Hey, David," Lance said, "this is Tracey, your date for the evening."

"Hello," David said, feeling a bit awkward.

"And this is Jennifer. Come on, let's get our seats and order some dinner," Lance said, leading the group into the theater.

The four of them found the show very entertaining. It turned out to be a mystery with a comedy twist. This was just the thing David needed, and he let himself forget about all concerns: stress at work, Danny's story, getting the lighthouse lit again, and Claire.

After the show, they decided to continue the evening at the North Star Bar.

"Claire," David said, as he quickly got out of bed to take the call in the other room.

"Hope I'm not calling at a bad time," she said.

David, thinking, *you have no idea*, but voicing instead, "No, you're not."

"I just had to call. I feel so bad about what I said to you when you called the other day."

"Don't. I understand," David said.

"You've been a good friend, I shouldn't have done that," she went on. "I don't think I've been myself lately. If you still need me to help you with your *Seahawk* story, I'm offering my services."

"What about Tyler?" David said, remembering what Lance had said regarding possible jealousy.

"Tyler and I broke up."

"You did?" David replied, trying to make sure his elation over hearing this news was not reflected in his voice.

"Yes, turns out he had applied for a transfer to Maine, and when he got it, he assumed I wanted to leave Stuart Cove and go with him."

"And I take it you didn't."

"Not at all. Besides, I'd noticed our relationship changing over the last few weeks, or maybe, it's me. Anyway, I just haven't felt comfortable."

David looked in his bedroom's direction. He felt guilty, even though he knew he should not.

"I don't have time to talk right now, but can I call you tomorrow? I have a lot to tell you," David said, as Tracey came walking in, clad in only her lace underwear.

"Okay, that'd be great," Claire said. "Talk to you then."

"Was that Lance?" Tracey asked, "Does he want to know if you scored last night?"

"Yea, what a lowlife he is," David responded.

"What's for breakfast?" she asked.

Feeling extremely uncomfortable, David just wanted to reverse the last fourteen hours somehow.

"I'm afraid I don't have much to offer." Tempted to give her a few bucks for breakfast down the street and get her out of his condo, he realized how that would look, so instead said, "Why don't you get dressed and I'll take you to Starbucks for breakfast?"

"Starbucks? You can do better than that, can't you?" she replied.

"I forgot I have an appointment I have to get to in about an hour, so we don't have time for anything else, I'm afraid," he said, hoping she would not question him further.

"In that case, I think I'll take a shower and go home," she said, turning and heading toward his bathroom.

Good, David thought, but feeling more like the *lowlife* he had accused Lance of being.

Later that afternoon, there was a knock at the door. *Please don't let it be Tracey*, David thought, walking to the door to look through the viewer.

"Why didn't you use your key?" David said, opening the door.

"I didn't want to take the chance of walking in on you and Tracey," Lance responded.

"Yea, well thanks a lot for setting up that date, buddy," David said sarcastically.

"What d'ya mean? I thought you two were getting along beautifully last night."

"Oh, we were. As a matter of fact, she stayed here last night."

"And you make that out as a bad thing?" Lance asked, smiling.

"It is a bad thing, Claire called me this morning."

"So?"

"So, she called to apologize for the phone call the other day and to say that she and Tyler broke up."

"Oh, I see. Bad timing, huh?" Lance said.

"I would say that," David replied, throwing a magazine at him.

Ducking, Lance said, "How the hell was I suppose to know that? I was just trying to look out for you, man;

figured you needed a diversion."

"So, what am I going to do if Tracey calls, or worse, comes over?"

"Tell her you have the hots for someone else. I'm sure she'll understand."

"Screw you!" David yelled.

***

"I'm not calling too early, am I?" David asked.

"No, not at all; I'm an early riser," Claire replied.

"I'm glad you called me yesterday. I'll have to admit, that last conversation we had surprised me."

"I'm really sorry for that."

"No worries, Claire. I have a lot to tell you. I met with a paranormal investigator about the mayday call. The guy's name is Owen Skinner."

"You did?" Claire asked, sounding very intrigued. "What did he say?"

"I was very impressed with the guy. He really seemed to know a lot about this sort of thing. Claire, you don't know how much it meant to talk to someone about it who understands."

"I can imagine," Claire said in a supporting tone.

"There is actually a category for that type of haunting."

"You're kidding."

"And, best of all, he has a solution. He wants us to turn the light back on."

"Turn it back on? How are we going to do that?" Claire responded. "It was deactivated back in 1956."

"I know; that's going to be the challenge."

"It's going to be more than a challenge; I don't see the historical society agreeing to this," Claire said.

"I figured that would be the case, so let's not even

111

ask. Owen knows a guy around here who's involved in lighthouse restorations. He contacted him to see if there was anyone in your area in that field. I just got an e-mail this morning. The guy's name is Emerson Hathaway, and he's in New Basewater. Is that close to you?"

"That's not far from here."

"I'm going to call him. He's already agreed to go to Stone Ridge and take a look; see what it's going to take to get her back on. Can you show him around without raising any suspicion?"

"I suppose I can. If anyone asks, I can tell them he's into that stuff and just wanted to get a more thorough tour," Claire replied.

"Great, I'll give the guy a call tonight."

David and Claire continued talking about the interview with Owen and made sure they exchanged e-mail addresses so they could keep in touch as the research and plans continued.

***

Claire was dusting the furniture in the dining room when Millie came in. "Mr. Emerson Hathaway is here to see you, Claire. Says he scheduled a special tour of the lighthouse with you."

Claire turned around to see a tall man who appeared to be in his late thirties, with shoulder-length salt-and-pepper hair. He wore jeans and a dark blue tee shirt.

"Hello, Emerson, let me put this away, and we'll get started."

"He already bought his ticket," Millie said, heading back to the gift shop.

"I'm sorry. She's such a stickler. I'll pay you back for that ticket."

"It's no problem. It goes to a good cause," Emerson

said.

"Yes, but you're doing us a favor by coming here and helping us with the light. I should at least pay your admission."

"Really, don't worry about it, Claire. Owen told me about your experience. I'm more than happy to do what I can to help you two out with this."

They walked through the kitchen and out the backdoor to the lighthouse.

"Have you been here before?" Claire asked.

"Actually, no, I'm embarrassed to say.

"You're here now, so you can add it to your lighthouse list."

They entered the lighthouse to find Jim at the counter, reading a book.

"Hi, folks," he said, putting the book aside.

"Hi, Jim, this is Emerson. I'm giving him a special tour. He's a friend of mine. Patrick is covering for me in the house while I show him around here."

"It's nice to meet you, Emerson. You have a top-notch guide there," Jim replied.

"Come on, I'll take you up to the lantern room," Claire said, as they began to climb the stairs. On their way up, they met a couple on the stairs, who were on their way down.

"Do you have any questions?" Claire asked the couple, as they allowed them to pass.

"No, but that sure was a great view," the man said, his wife agreeing with the statement.

They continued their ascent up the stairs to the lens room where Emerson immediately examined the area. Claire stood back, leaving Emerson to his work.

"I need to see the clock mechanism," he finally said.

"Okay, follow me," Claire replied, taking him down

into the office.

"Is that the radio?" Emerson asked, noticing the channel receiver sitting on the table.

"Yes, it is," Claire responded.

Shaking his head, he added, "That must have been some experience." Then, turning his attention to the lens pedestal located in the center of the room, he watched Claire open the panel.

"Here it is," she said, showing him the clock mechanism.

"That's what I need to look at," he said, studying the machinery and taking notes in a small notebook he pulled out of his breast pocket.

Claire looked over his shoulder but kept quiet, allowing him to concentrate on the business at hand. After a few minutes, Claire heard the footsteps of visitors approaching. As they entered the room, she very tactfully guided them around the room to avoid interfering with Emerson. She then took them up to the lens room where she kept their attention answering questions, allowing him to complete his examination.

"This is one beautiful prism, isn't it?" Emerson asked, joining the group in the lens room. The questions and answers continued, with Emerson sharing his knowledge with the group. Once the visitors were satisfied, they thanked their guides and headed down the spiral staircase.

"I think I have all the information I need." Emerson paused. "I expect you don't want to talk about this here?

"No, that wouldn't be a good idea," Claire replied.

"I was planning to meet up with a friend in town for a while. Maybe later, we can meet there. When do you get off work?"

"I'll be getting off at three. How about we meet at the Fishhook Pub at half past three? Do you know where that is?" Claire asked.

"I think I do, but the guy I'm meeting is from here, so he should know."

"So, are we going to be able to pull this off?" Claire asked, anxious to know the answer.

"It's going to be a bit of a challenge, but I think so. We'll talk more about it later," Emerson answered.

"Great, so I'll see you then, and thanks again for helping us out with this."

"Hey, this sounds like a pretty interesting case you guys got yourselves into."

After Emerson left, Claire went back into the house to relieve Patrick. She found him in the gift shop, talking to Millie.

"You and your friend received rave compliments from the last group that was here," Patrick said.

"Really," Claire responded.

"Yea, they said they learned more about lighthouses during that tour then they ever had at any other lighthouse."

***

Claire walked into the Fishhook Pub to find Emerson sitting by himself in a booth.

"I see you found the place," Claire said, sliding onto the bench across from him.

"Yea, not hard to find," he said, sipping his beer.

Mary approached the table. "Hi, Claire, sorry to hear about you and Tyler."

"Ah, it was for the best," Claire replied.

Emerson ran his finger down the condensation on the glass, as they talked.

"You were too good for him, anyway," Mary said with a wink. "Can I get you something to wet your whistle?"

"I'll take an iced tea."

As soon as Mary departed, Claire turned her attention to Emerson. "So, what's the verdict?"

"As you might have noticed, they've pretty much destroyed the wiring, so that rules out electricity. We're going to have to get her lit the old-fashioned way, by using the clock works.

"Can you get that working?" Claire asked.

"I better make it clear right now; I'm not interested in working on it without the proper permission. It's one thing to look at it with your giving me a *special tour*; it's a whole nuther thing me actually working on it without them knowing."

Claire's expression of excitement over the thought of getting their plan in order was now replaced with disappointment.

"So, we're screwed," she said, frowning.

"Not necessarily; how's David's mechanical ability?"

"Geeze, I don't really know," she thought a moment. "I know he was doing a lot of work on his aunt's house, which included fixing things," she said.

"I took a good look at the mechanism, and I think I know what it will take to get it working. It's going to need some parts, which I should be able to get, but it will take me a little time. I'd imagine David will be able to make the necessary repairs with some instruction. Luckily, it's in pretty good shape."

Mary brought the iced tea.

"Would you two like anything to eat?"

"No, I think we're fine," Claire said, as she gave a questioning look at Emerson.

"No," Emerson added, holding his hand up.

"So, do you think we're crazy?" Claire said, as soon

116

as Mary was out of earshot.

"Hell, no," Emerson replied. "I'm familiar with Owen and the work he does. I'm not sure why, but lighthouses seem to attract that sort of thing. I've heard enough stories and even experienced bumps in the night on my travels, working on these structures.

"Really?" Claire said, fascinated by his candidness.

"Nothing like your story, of course," he added.

"I didn't experience the mayday call, but I did see David right afterward, and he had a look in his eyes I don't think I can ever forget. Seeing the entries in the log was pretty creepy too."

"I bet it was."

"So, what's going to happen if we get her lit again?" Claire asked.

"I can't tell you that; you'll have to ask Owen. He's the expert there. Maybe it will allow them to move on. Maybe they're stuck between here and there—whatever that means."

"I can't quite get my mind around that. I'm still not sure what I believe and what I don't," Claire said.

"I guess that's what makes it so exciting to some people—people like Owen. Part of what they try to do is get answers to these questions."

Claire stopped and looked into her glass. Thinking about the concept, she tried to grasp what it was they were trying to do.

"We'll get this puppy lit; don't worry. Then, the spirits will be happy, and all will be right with the world," Emerson said with a smile.

Claire looked up and chuckled.

"Hope you're right."

***

It was Monday morning at work. David was attempting to compile his article entitled *Avoiding the Morning Rush*, when he found himself instead distracted by the conversation he had with Claire the day before. He was excited about the thought of getting the lighthouse lit again and a little concerned about his ability to carry out the job. *If only I could go there right now and check it out*, David thought. The fact was he would have to wait until July, right before the anniversary of the storm.

"Hey, David, you interested in going to the Transit Club next week for Halloween?" Julie asked, approaching David's desk, followed closely by Sam.

Aside from seeing Lance regularly, David's social life had become nonexistent, notably since his encounter with Tracey.

"Oh, I don't know," David responded, surprised by his own response.

"Come on, it'll be fun. Besides, you haven't been out with us in a while," Sam said.

"You know I've been busy here."

"Yea, and we also know they give you some time off," Julie responded.

"I'll think about it and let you know later in the week. How's that?"

"If that's the best you can do, then I guess we have to go with that," Julie said, giving David a playful slap on the back as they left.

About this time, David became aware that he was changing. What he did not realize, nor could he control, was how profound the change was. It not only affected his interests, but also his principles, reaching his very core. The process was slow, making it difficult for him to fully recognize, yet.

Chapter Eight

It was Friday evening when Lance knocked two times, and then using his key, unlocked the front door of David's condo.

"Anybody home?" Lance said, walking in.

"In here," David called back.

Lance went into David's bedroom and found him packing a small suitcase.

"Hey, man, whatcha doing?" Lance asked.

David turned and answered, "I'm outta here for the weekend. Claire and some friends invited me to go with them to Salem tomorrow. I'm leaving tonight to meet them in Connecticut."

"That's cool. So, you'll be there till Sunday?"

"That's the plan, man," he said, turning his attention back to packing. At that moment, the phone rang.

"That's probably Claire," David said, walking around the bed to answer the phone from the bedside table.

"I'll raid your fridge while you're busy on the phone."

Lance left David and went into the kitchen to check out the food situation. He opened the refrigerator to find a six-pack, half a loaf of whole wheat bread, three eggs, half a jar of grape jelly, and some butter. Lance, realizing these offerings were not about to satisfy his hunger, headed back to David's bedroom to complain about the situation. He stopped at the bedroom door and realized from this end of the conversation that it was not Claire who had called.

"Shit!" David said, hanging up the phone.

"I take it that was not Claire."

"No, it was not. It looks like I will not be going to

Connecticut after all. I have to work."

"That's a bum deal. Isn't there any way you can get out of it?" Lance asked.

"Not a chance. You know about that uproar in the Gatten neighborhood where they want to tear down the community center and build a hotel?"

"Sure I do; it's been all over the news," Lance answered.

"I've been working on a story that will allege one of the city planning commissioners took a very large bribe to see that hotel gets built. I was just about to release the story. That was Russ on the phone. He tells me our source was just killed in an elevator accident."

"Damn. Where did it happen?"

"The building where he works, on Chase Avenue. It happened about thirty minutes ago," David said, abandoning his packing and instead quickly changing into his work clothes.

Do you think it was a coincidence?" Lance asked.

"Don't know, but it looks like I have to get over there and find out."

"Bad timing for you," Lance added.

"Yea, couldn't the guy have waited until Monday?" David said sarcastically.

"By the way, you don't have shit in your fridge to eat."

Gathering up his laptop, David said, "If you recall, I wasn't planning on being here."

"Hey, don't forget to call Claire to let her know."

"I'll call her on the way. I've got to get outta here."

"Sorry, guy, looks like your plans got screwed up again."

"Thanks for the sympathy," David replied, rushing out the door. Then calling back, he added, "Don't forget to lock up when you leave."

David could sense from Claire's tone that she was disappointed he would not be able to join them for the weekend, which only added to his own disappointment, but he had to put that aside and turn his attention to his job.

"I'll get out here," David said to the taxi driver who was finding it difficult to approach 1536 Chase Avenue because of the emergency vehicles. He got out of the taxi and walked the rest of the way to the building. As David approached, a police officer stopped him.

"I'm afraid you cannot enter the building, sir."

As David was attempting to retrieve his press badge from the inside pocket of his jacket, Russ came out of the building.

"It's okay; he's with me."

The officer then waved David in where he joined Russ, and the two of them entered the building through one of the massive glass doors.

The lobby displayed a contemporary design of off-white marble floors and dark gray marble walls. A theme of squares and rectangles surrounded the light fixtures and building information signs in both marble and teak. A dark cherry wood table in the middle of the floor held a tall glass vase of yellow oncidium orchids, dark purple calla lilies, bird of paradise, and philodendron leaves. Located at the far end of the lobby was a teak reception desk, now busy with activity.

"What have you been able to find out?" David asked, as they made their way through the lobby toward the bank of elevators.

"Looks like it dropped from the eighth floor—broke his neck."

The walls of the elevator lobby were teak. Two elevators on each side of the hall were surrounded by dark gray marble, carrying the theme from the main lobby. The doors of each elevator were brass. The far left door was open, and the body of their source, Jason McDowell, was lying on the elevator floor, now covered by a tarp while the officers continued collecting possible evidence.

As David and Russ stood a short distance from the open door, Detective Burke approached them.

"Parker, your boy Russ tells me you might have some information that could turn this accident investigation into a homicide investigation. You notice you two are the only press personnel here? What d'ya have for me?"

"Yes, I did notice that, detective; appreciate it. Let's talk in the lobby."

The three of them left the area of the elevators and went to a far corner of the lobby away from other personnel.

"Your victim is a source who provided information for a bribery article I was about to release," David explained.

"Do you have any proof someone was after him?" the detective asked.

"No, I don't."

"Look, that is interesting information, but until we can prove otherwise, this is an accident," the detective sternly replied. He added, "We have the building inspectors looking at it right now to determine the cause for the failure."

"I did a story a while back about another elevator accident. Unless it is because of faulty maintenance, it is unlikely the multiple safety backups would all fail."

"So, Parker, what makes you think the maintenance work here couldn't have been shabby?" Detective Burke asked.

"Just keeping an open mind," David replied.

"No harm in that, I suppose. Now, I have to get back to work. You guys try to stay out of the way," the detective said, as he left David and Russ and headed back to the elevators.

"What time did this happen?" David asked Russ.

"It happened at ten after five. He was leaving his office for the day."

"Does he always leave at that time?"

"The security guy wouldn't give me that information," Russ replied.

"I think we got everything we can from here. Let's go back to the office. We have some phone calls to make."

The body was being rolled out toward the front door where an ambulance was waiting. A crowd had collected at the entrance of the building, making it difficult for David and Russ to leave the scene.

Once back at the office, David began gathering the information he had on the previous elevator accident. He kept an electronic Rolodex on each previous contact he had and added to this other contacts he gathered from reading articles or books. More than once he found this useful for future stories. After a few minutes of research, he was able to locate the name of the elevator inspector he had talked to the year before. Looking at his watch, David saw it was 6:45 and figured it would be a long shot trying to reach the guy at work this time of day. He noticed his message light blinking when he picked up the phone but decided to try calling the guy first before checking it. After four rings, the voice mail message began. David left a message for him to call as soon as he got into work, stating it was urgent. Discouraged, he played back the messages from his voice mail.

"You have three messages. First message received at three thirty p.m.. David, this is Jason McDowell. I would have called you on your cell phone, but I lost the number. I wanted to let you know that I received a call from a man who wouldn't give me his name, said I better not talk to the police about the information I had. Before I received that call, I had suspected someone might be following me. I'm really worried and not sure what to do. Call me as soon as you get this."

"Russ, get over here," David yelled, still holding the receiver in his hand.

"Whatcha got?" Russ asked, approaching David's desk.

"It seems our source called me shortly before his *so called* accident. Listen to this. David put it on speaker and replayed the message.

"That could be our evidence," Russ said.

David handed Russ a piece of paper with the name Tim Bragg on it. "Find this guy's home phone number. He's the elevator inspector we need to talk to. Also, contact people from McDowell's office and try to find out what his normal schedule was, if he had a consistent schedule.

Shortly after David located his files pertaining to the previous elevator accident, Russ came by with the phone number.

"Here it is. You want me to call him?"

"No, I'll give him a call, thanks," David said, taking the piece of paper from Russ. Moments later, he had Tim on the phone. He gave him what information he had about the accident, not mentioning the connection with the victim.

"Can you find out what the safety record is for those elevators?" David asked.

"Sure, do you suspect a problem?" Tim asked.

"Yes, I do, and I'd like to be the first to expose it."

"Understand; I can probably have that information

by tomorrow morning."

After David gave Tim his cell phone number, he went back to his research.

"We need to tell Detective Burke about the voice mail," Russ said. "We'll go by and talk to him in the morning. Maybe I can talk him into exchanging some information."

It was nine o'clock by the time David left the office Friday evening. Knowing his refrigerator was absent of any sort of meal, he stopped by the Imperial Inn for take-out. Later, as he sat in his kitchen eating his egg roll and beef with mixed vegetables, he thought about his missed weekend with Claire and her friends. He realized it could not have been helped, but this did not prevent the disappointment he felt. He was especially troubled that he had assured Claire he would be there to offer support, knowing she was apprehensive about going to a place so anchored in the paranormal. These thoughts plagued him into the night, until he fell asleep.

***

David and Russ were back in the office by seven the following morning. Shortly after their arrival, David received a phone call from Tim.

"Tim, glad to hear from you. Do you have something for me?" David asked.

"Those elevators check out. They are Wright elevators, both installed and maintained by the company. The company has a great reputation and safety record. I personally checked the safety record and the maintenance schedule for those elevators. Their record is excellent, and they are regularly maintained. The yearly city inspection was done last month, and they passed."

"Thanks, Tim. I owe you lunch."

"And I'm gonna hold you to it," Tim replied.

After hanging up the phone, David found Russ at his desk. "Come on, we have to go to the Sixth Precinct to talk to Detective Burke."

"How do you know he's there?" Russ asked, quickly grabbing his portfolio.

"I know because I just talked to him. I also arranged for you to talk to Detective Simms about that evidence room story you're working on. Come on."

They arrived by eight, but both detectives were unavailable, causing David and Russ to wait. They joined others in the waiting area: a chubby middle-aged man reading a car magazine; a very thin young woman with a nose ring, wearing tight jeans and a black tank top under a leather jacket; and an elderly woman reading a book. At the front desk, an officer was busy answering the phone and filling out paperwork. They continued to wait for what seemed like an hour, which, in reality, was twenty-five minutes.

"I thought you said he was expecting us," Russ said to David in frustration.

"Patience—that's what you need in this business, a lot of patience," David responded. At that moment, Detective Burke came into the room.

"Sorry to keep you guys waiting. Follow me."

They followed him around the reception desk and down the hallway to the office he shared with another detective.

"Thompson's not here, so we'll just borrow his chair," Burke said, grabbing the visitor's chair from his office mate's area and placing it next to his own visitor chair. David and Russ took their seats, Russ noticing the disarray of papers and folders on Detective Burke's desk. It appeared as if someone had just thrown them there to fall where they might. This was quiet opposite to Russ's desk. He had everything placed in its proper receptacle, organized and ready for retrieval. He knew where everything was and took pride in that fact.

"You told me on the phone you have more information to share about your source," Detective Burke said, leaning back in his chair.

"Yes, I do," David said, and he proceeded to relay the message he had on his voice mail.

Hearing this, the detective changed his manner and became most interested. "Can I get a copy of that recording?" he asked.

"I have it right here on my digital recorder. It has a USB port; you can load it on your computer if you like," David said.

"I don't know how to do that shit. Here, you do it," Detective Burke said, moving out of the way, so David could sit at his desk.

After David set up a directory on his computer and copied the WMA audio file to the directory, he put away his recorder and returned to the visitor chair.

"I understand you have some information for me," David said.

"Yes, we got our preliminary report back from the inspectors this morning. They were working through the night on this," Detective Burke answered. "It shows someone might have tampered with the friction clamp safety. Are you familiar with what that does?"

"Yes," replied David. "It is meant to slow the elevator down if it should reach a speed higher than that set for the bank of cars, which usually depends on the distance they have to go."

"That's right; thing is there are other safety features that should have kicked in as well, but did not. They're still looking into that. I think we have enough here to turn this investigation toward a new direction," the detective added.

"I can only agree," David replied.

The headline from Monday's edition of the *New York Daily Press* read: "SUSPECTED BRIBERY CAUSE OF GATTEN COMMUNITY CENTER DESTRUCTION — Source Dies in Suspicious Elevator Accident."

Chapter Nine

Placing his cards on the table, Dawson smiled, "I think my *straight* beats your *three of a kind*, Miss Claire."

"You did it again. I thought for sure I had you beat this time," Claire said, counting her remaining chips.

Sean was shuffling the cards when Claire's cell phone rang. She grabbed it out of her purse and noticed it was David calling.

"Deal me out; it's David," Claire said, getting up from her chair to take the call in the next room.

"You better deal me a better hand this time," Kay said, as she collected her cards.

"It's not just the cards, but what you do with what you get," said Dawson.

"So, what did you get to feed us? I'm getting hungry," Kay asked.

"Hey, I'm supplying the location and the beer. Aren't you guys supposed to supply the food?" Dawson replied.

Placing his discarded cards on the table, Sean said, "That's not what I heard. If it's your house, it has to be your food as well."

Claire came back to the dining room, looking a bit forlorn.

"What's the matter?" asked Kay.

"That was David; looks like he won't be coming with us tomorrow. He has to work."

"That sucks; no way he can get out of it?" Sean asked.

"No, he didn't want to go into it, but he mentioned he had to deal with it personally. Something happened relating to an article he was about to release."

Claire was a bit surprised and even concerned that

she felt this disappointed he could not make it. In an attempt to conceal her feelings, she put on a smile and took her seat back at the table.

"Deal me in, and let's order some pizza."

The friends proceeded to play cards and eat pizza into the evening.

***

It was cool enough for jackets this fall morning, as Kay and Claire waited in front of their house for the guys to pick them up. Claire sat on the steps to the front door, her hands wrapped around her coffee cup, trying to get warm.

"Wish I got a little more sleep," Kay said, standing over Claire, her hands in her pockets.

"Yea, we probably should have stopped that game a little sooner than we did."

"You know how Dawson is. As long as he's winning, he wants to keep playing."

"About time," Kay said, seeing Dawson driving up the street. He pulled in their driveway in his two-door Nissan Skyline.

"Good morning, ladies," he said, as he and Sean got out of the car, so Kay and Claire could climb in the backseat.

"To Salem, driver," Sean said once everyone was in the car and they were on their way.

"What's our itinerary?" asked Dawson.

"Based on our conversation the other day, and knowing you guys would not do your own research, Kay and I went online and came up with some ideas."

"Great, and you're right, we didn't do crap to prepare for this."

As they made their way to I-95, Claire said, "We'll

start at the Old Burying Point Cemetery. That's supposed to be the second oldest burial ground in the United States. Some people accused of witchcraft are buried there. After that, Kay and I are going to attend a mock witch trial while you two go to the House of the Living Dead."

"Hey, that sounds cool," Sean responded.

"Yea, I figured you guys wouldn't be interested in the trial, and I KNOW we aren't interested in that place. They're not far from each other, so you can drop us off," Claire said, handing Sean the map.

"Next, we're going to visit the Stuart House. He's a ship captain related to our Captain George Stuart of Stuart Cove. I've wanted to go there for years. Course, if you guys think that's too boring, you can find something else to do while I'm there," Claire said.

"That's fine. We can all go; it won't kill us," Kay responded.

"Sounds like a plan to me," Dawson added.

They continued their drive to Massachusetts. The steady sound of the engine and traffic soon put Kay to sleep. The guys talked between themselves, and Claire, toning out their conversation, sat quietly looking out the side window. She admired the trees—how they had transformed into the vibrant oranges, reds, and yellows of the season. As the sun continued its ascent, the light illuminated the yellow foliage, turning it a brilliant gold. It would not be long before the trees would give up their treasures, leaving the branches bare until spring.

Claire, although looking forward to their day in Salem, was slightly apprehensive. She had never taken ghost stories, scary movies, or the observance of Halloween seriously, but after the experience David had with the radio, her view of the paranormal had changed. It had become more real to her. She felt slightly angry that David was not going to be here, as he had promised, for he was the one person she could talk to about these feelings. Little did her friends realize that if they were looking for October ghosts, they need not go any further than the Stone Ridge Lighthouse. They continued their drive, stopping once to get gas, stretch their legs, and pick up some snacks.

As they entered Salem, Sean began navigating, directing Dawson to the Old Burying Point Cemetery. After finding a place to park the car, the four of them walked to the cemetery.

"This place is pretty creepy," Kay said, as they entered the grounds. They soon spread out, each reading different headstones. It was not laid out as modern cemeteries are with rows of fancy marble headstones. Instead, it contained mostly simple thin headstones, some of which had not fared well over the years and were now cracked.

"Over here," Sean yelled, "look at this one."

They joined Sean at the gravesite reading *BRIDGET BISHOP, HANGED, JUNE 10, 1692.*

"She was one of the accused witches hanged on Gallows Hill," Claire said.

"Makes you sad, doesn't it?" Kay said.

They continued to wander around the grounds, each occasionally pointing out a headstone for the others to view.

"Okay, I think I've had enough of this place," Dawson said to Sean. "Let's get the girls and get outta here."

The four of them left the cemetery and went back to the car, and Sean went back to navigating.

"I think that's it," Claire said, as they passed a dark gray building. Dawson quickly pulled over.

"I'll run in and find out when the next trial is," Claire said, as Sean got out of the car to let her out.

"Sure glad you two didn't sign us up for this one," Dawson said.

"Afraid you might learn something?" Kay shot back.

Claire came running back to the car. "Come on; let's go. The next one is in seven minutes."

"Couldn't have timed that any better," Sean said. "When should we come back and get you?"

"This is about an hour long. Call us when you're done."

Claire and Kay then rushed inside, arriving just in time before the doors of the mock courtroom were closed. At the far end of the room, atop a short platform, was a long table where the judges were to preside over the trial. A long green cloth draped over this table, reaching the floor. Leading up to the platform was an aisle, with three long benches on either side, positioned at a slight angle toward the judges' table. Seven men sat at the table, all dressed in black robes, all with stern looks. Claire and Kay sat together on a bench located toward the back of the courtroom. Suddenly, the doors opened and a man in period dress entered.

"Ladies and gentlemen, may I have your attention? You are about to witness the trial of Mary Easty; she is accused of witchcraft. You, the jury will decide, based on the testimony you will hear, whether she is guilty."

At that moment, they heard a woman's screams. She appeared at the door, fighting against the two men bringing her in the courtroom. They were all in character and dressed in the 17th-century attire.

Tugging at Kay's sleeve, Claire whispered in her ear, "This is exciting."

Claire and Kay watched the trial and participated in the questioning, as others did in the audience.

"Ladies and gentlemen of the jury, you have just

133

heard the testimony; it is now time for your decision. Who here finds Mary Easty guilty of witchcraft?"

More than half the audience raised their hands.

"Mary Easty, please stand to hear the verdict." The two men, one on each side, grabbed her arms and forced her to stand.

He continued, "Mary Easty, you have been found guilty of witchcraft. You are now sentenced to death by hanging."

The woman screamed at the audience, as she was forcefully led out of the courtroom. "You just wait. You, too, may be accused of this crime."

As soon as she left the courtroom, the audience broke out in applause.

"That was fun," Kay said to Claire, as they joined the others in exiting the room.

"I told you you'd like it," Claire responded. "A cousin of mine went to one of these in Virginia last year. She loved it.

They met up with Sean and Dawson later for lunch at a nearby deli where they shared their courtroom experience in detail with the guys.

"I'd rather take part in the hanging than the trial," said Dawson, as they finished up their lunch.

"You're just morbid," Kay responded.

"What d'ya expect? They just finished going through the House of the Living Dead," Claire added.

Once back in the car, Sean navigated them to the Stuart House where they were able to park in the small parking lot next to the house.

"I appreciate you all coming with me on this tour. I know it's not your favorite thing to do," Claire said, as they walked toward the house together.

"Yea, what we do for you," Sean said jokingly, as Kay pushed him.

They approached the black front door of the white Federal-style home where two women were speaking to each other.

"Welcome to the Stuart House. Will you be joining us on a tour today?" one woman asked.

"Yes, we are," Claire responded.

"Would you mind walking around the side to the carriage house where you can purchase your tickets?"

The group, following her direction, walked along to the side of the house where they first examined a 1920 Pierce Arrow touring car parked inside the carriage house.

"Don't see these every day," Dawson said.

They proceeded to the counter where a man with white hair and a round cheerful face sold them their tickets and gave them each a small leaflet explaining the house's history. With tickets now in hand, they again met the well-dressed woman at the front door.

"Please follow me," the woman said, opening the front door leading into the main entrance foyer. Once everyone stepped into the foyer, she proceeded to relay the home's history.

"This is the Stuart House, which was built in 1783. Captain Jacob Stuart and his family originally owned it. Salem was once one of the most significant ports in the nation. Captain Stuart made a fine living in international trade, particularly with the Far East. The wealth he obtained is reflected in his home."

"Yes, it certainly is," Sean commented.

A slender man dressed in a light tan suit entered the foyer. "Hello, my name is Timothy. I will be taking you through the rest of the house."

"Enjoy your tour," the woman said, and then left through the front door.

The group proceeded through the house, examining

the rooms and listening to Timothy explain the importance of items and share what he knew of the Stuart family. As they were touring the upstairs, they passed a room that was obviously a child's room.

"This was Ann's room. She was the oldest of the Stuart's three children."

The room was beautifully decorated, as was the rest of the house. There was a rocking horse in the corner, and in the opposite corner, a doll sat on a small chair. Other early American toys lay on the bed, as if she had just finished playing with them. Claire suddenly felt uncomfortable, and goose bumps emerged on her arms.

Timothy continued, "When Ann grew to adulthood, they say she was able to speak to those who had passed. Now, as you can imagine, that did not go over well in Salem. It was around that time that the family moved to Connecticut."

"Where in Connecticut?" Claire asked, concern in her voice.

"Actually, I'm not sure," Timothy answered, and not giving it a second thought, proceeded to the next bedroom.

Claire stood there a moment, not sure what to think and why she felt as she did.

"You all right?" Kay asked, noticing Claire was acting odd. "Do you think they moved to Stuart Cove?"

"Don't know," Claire responded, then brushing it off, she followed the group through the rest of the house.

After visiting the Stuart House, they spent some time in town, had dinner, and stuck around long enough to go on a candlelight tour. It was ten at night by the time they got back to Stuart Cove.

***

"Don't you miss the snow, Mom?" Claire asked, standing at the sink washing the dishes while her mother prepared the turkey.

"Not a bit, but I do miss the New England falls."

It was now customary for Claire to come visit her mother in Florida each Christmas. Her aunts, uncles, and cousins sometimes joined her. Claire enjoyed this time she spent with her family, but the yearning she felt for those Christmases of her childhood in Stuart Cove, Connecticut, never seemed to pass.

"Can you hand me that bowl, honey?"

"Is Uncle Steven going to make it here this year?" Claire asked, handing her the bowl.

"I'm expecting him."

"You know he's going to ask me about Tyler. He'll probably give me a hard time about us breaking up, and only because that means he lost a golfing buddy."

"If you ask me, and you didn't, I think it's a good thing you're no longer with him," Claire's mother said.

"I didn't know you felt that way, Mom."

"He seemed to be a bit overbearing. I always felt he was jealous of your interests."

"Mom, you're very observant. I finally came to realize that myself. I guess it just took me a little longer, though."

"You seem to be holding up well," her mother commented.

"Yea, that surprised me. I thought I'd be more upset than I was. That just goes to show it was meant to be; and besides, I've been able to get more schoolwork done since we broke up. I have a couple of very tough classes coming up next semester, so not having a guy in my life will be a benefit."

Cindy, Claire's six-year-old cousin, came into the kitchen with an empty plate in her hands.

"Daddy finished his sandwich," she said, handing the plate to Claire.

"Thank you for bringing us his empty plate. Are you still watching the Christmas movie?"

"Yes, and I saw a parade with Santa Claus." She then ran back into the living room to join her parents.

"She get's prettier every year," Claire commented.

"Now, what about the young man you were telling me about earlier—David?"

Turning her attention back to their conversation, Claire said, "He's just a friend of mine I met last June. We've been working on a research project together for an article he's writing."

"You met him back in June? How long does it take to write an article?" Claire's mother asked.

"It's complicated. It's probably going to start out as an article, and then be a short story about a past lighthouse keeper from my lighthouse. He lives in New York. I think his title is investigative reporter, works at the *New York Daily Press*. His life is very different from mine."

"That might be true, but you've mentioned him a few times since you've been here, and I see a sparkle in your eyes when you do."

"Mom, I've told you; this is not a relationship I am interested in, and I have a lot of school to get through."

"What's that sound?" her mother asked.

"That's my cell phone," Claire answered, digging through her purse at the kitchen table to retrieve it. She looked at the phone, then smiled and looked at her mother, "It's David."

Her mother smiled back and continued preparing the Christmas dinner.

Chapter Ten

Approaching the last houses on the dead-end road, David noticed a small dark gray Cape Cod nestled behind a row of Eastern white pine. He pulled into Claire's driveway. Closer examination of the house with its shake-shingle siding revealed it was in need of a fresh coat of paint. A brick walkway cut through the recently cut lawn to the Yale blue front door. There were windows on each side of the entrance, both in danger of being taken over by the growth of the box hedge planted many years ago, but rarely trimmed. Hanging from the front wall light were two red-and-green crabpot-marker buoys, faded by the sun.

David approached the front entrance, but just as he raised his hand to take hold of the doorknocker, Claire swung the door open and gave him a strong hug.

"Wow, I didn't expect that," he said, returning the embrace.

"I'm glad to see you, David. Come in."

He stepped into the foyer, where the steps leading to the second floor were in front of him. He felt something against his leg, and looking down, he saw a large black-striped tabby.

"That's my baby, Sam," Claire said, reaching down to pet his head.

"I hope you're not allergic to cats."

"No," he said, carefully walking around Sam, as Claire led him into the large living room.

The place had a cozy, feminine atmosphere. The furniture was a mismatch of styles. In the center of the room was a dark brown leather sofa, in front of which was a glass-top coffee table. Sitting catty corner to this arrangement was a plaid overstuffed chair. The floor, a dark hardwood, was partially covered by a Persian-style rug. David noticed a large framed poster of New England lighthouses on the wall. In a corner of the living room, between two bookcases, there was a computer desk, the type of desk you would find at an office supply store. This reminded David of the time he purchased a similar desk. It came in multiple boxes and took him two hours to assemble, only to find there were parts missing.

"It's a nice place you have here."

"I like it, but since Kay moved out, it's been a struggle meeting the rent with my part-time salary. I think I'm going to have to find another roommate."

Pointing to the backdoor, Claire mentioned, "Please be careful; Sam is a housecat, but that doesn't stop him from trying to get out if you give him a chance."

"I appreciate your letting me stay here while I'm in town."

"It's no problem at all; come, I'll show you your room," Claire said, leading David through the living room, past the kitchen, and to the first-floor bedroom. As they passed the bathroom, Claire opened the door. "This is your bathroom."

"Okay."

"And this will be your room; hope it'll suffice."

"Of course it will Claire; it's fine," David said, placing his suitcase on the double brass bed positioned with its headboard against the wall.

"You unpack while I get us some lunch. Ham and cheese okay?" Claire asked over her shoulder as she headed back toward the kitchen.

"That sounds great; I'm starved."

Sam, who had followed him into the room, jumped on the bed and began rubbing up against David's suitcase, claiming it as his own. David reached over and scratched Sam behind the ears, and he purred in delight.

Looking around the room, he noticed it was sparsely furnished. Besides the bed, a wooden crate served the purpose of a bedside table. On it was a small reading lamp. Opposite the bed was a small chest-of-drawers. A window in the room looked out on a field. The house sat catty-corner on the lot of the dead-end road. David, noticing how quiet it was, thought, *I'm back in Stuart Cove*, and a sense of tranquility came over him. After unpacking his suitcase, he went to join Claire in the kitchen.

"Thanks again," David said.

"It's really nothing. You don't have to keep thanking me. Have a seat," Claire said, motioning David to a barstool where the kitchen opened up to the living room through a counter area.

"Here ya go. Nothing fancy, but it should satisfy your hunger," Claire said, placing the plate in front of him.

"Iced tea?" she asked.

"That would be great, thanks. So, when are we supposed to meet Emerson?"

"We have a meeting set up for eleven o'clock tomorrow. We're supposed to meet him at the Sentinel Lighthouse."

"Where's that?" David asked, as Claire joined him at the kitchen bar.

"It's in the town of New Basewater, a bit of a drive, about fifty miles west. We should plan to leave about nine-thirty."

"I'm glad we're not going electrical," David said. "I'm not crazy about the thought of electrifying myself in this endeavor."

"No, that would be difficult to explain," she replied.

"Oh, that's it, difficult to explain. How about me, lying dead on the floor?"

"There is that, too, I guess," Claire said with a smile.

Once they finished their lunch, Claire cleared the dishes.

"I hope you don't mind, but I have an errand to take care of. I need to go see Ellen," David said.

"That's right; it's almost been a year. Are your renters planning on extending their lease?"

"That's what I need to talk to Ellen about. Last we heard, they weren't sure. Mr. Gately's job might be transferring him."

"Gosh, I hope not. Otherwise, you'll have to deal with finding renters again. Unless, of course, you want to sell it," Claire said, finishing up the dishes.

"One step at a time; first, I have to find out what the Gatelys are planning."

"I have to get to my afternoon class, anyway," Claire said, as she went into the living room and began loading her backpack with books. "Here's an extra key. I should be back around six o'clock. I was going to make spaghetti tonight. Should I plan on your appearance?"

"You sure can," David responded.

***

As David woke up, he noticed a gentle rain was falling outside. It had a calming effect, as he lay there listening. He was glad to be back in Stuart Cove and especially grateful to be back in Claire's company.

"Did you bring a rain coat?" Claire asked, as David joined her in the kitchen.

"No, afraid I didn't."

"It's only a light rain, and it's supposed to stop some time later in the morning, so maybe you'll be okay. Would you like some coffee?"

"Music to my ears," David responded, taking the coffee cup from Claire.

"What do you take in your coffee?" she asked.

"Nothing, I like it black; this is fine just the way it is," he said, taking a sip.

"I thought I'd make breakfast for us, since we have a little bit of a drive this morning. How about a ham-and-cheese omelet with fresh tomatoes and toast on the side?"

"You're spoiling me, Claire. I'm going to have to pay you back. I'll cook my specialty dish for you."

"And what is that?" she asked.

"Steak on the grill."

"That's your specialty dish?" she responded with a smile.

"Well, yea, afraid my cooking talent is limited, but I do make a damn good steak."

"I'll take you up on that, maybe this evening. I have a grill in the backyard."

"Deal," David said, as he began slicing the tomato while she assembled the omelet.

The light but constant rain continued as they drove to New Basewater.

"So, you were impressed with Emerson?" David asked.

"Yea, he seems to really know his stuff."

"I hope so, 'cause we don't have much time for a plan B if this doesn't work," David replied.

"I don't think we have to worry about that."

"Famous last words," David responded. "Sorry for sounding so pessimistic, but this plan really needs to fall into place without a hitch."

The wiper blades of Claire's '96 Civic went back and forth in a rhythmic pattern, as she drove up the highway.

"I think you'll be impressed with him."

They found the parking lot of the Sentinel Lighthouse about two-thirds full this Saturday morning.

"I'm glad to see this place is popular," Claire said, pulling into an empty spot. "That usually means the place is getting the support it needs to stay open."

Looking at her watch, Claire said, "We made good time; it's only half past ten."

"Where are we supposed to meet him?"

"At the museum," Claire responded and added, "Perfect, it looks like the rain has stopped." Quickly getting out of the car, she said, "Come on, let's check out the lighthouse. You up for a climb? This one has 269 stairs." There was joy in her voice, as she said this. It made David feel good to see her excitement. She was obviously in her element. "Sure, I'm game; let's go."

They went into the large gift shop where the tickets were sold and where the entrance to the lighthouse station was.

"This is on me," David said, as they approached the counter, reaching for his wallet.

"Well, thank you," Claire responded, as she bowed her head in appreciation.

They exited the gift shop and entered a large courtyard. In the middle of the courtyard stood the 210-foot lighthouse, the day mark of the tall tower displayed bands of white, then red, then white again. On the outskirts of the courtyard were buildings of various sizes. Homes on either side used to be occupied by past lighthouse keepers' families. There was a fog signal building, a brick oil hut, and other outbuildings.

"Isn't she a beauty," Claire said, as she tilted her head back to admire the tall structure.

"She sure is," David answered, knowing it was more a comment than a question. As he watched her, he found himself admiring her enthusiasm, even more than the lighthouse. The sun emerged from the clouds, as they entered the tower.

Claire stood at the bottom of the staircase and looked upward through the spiral, "David, come here; I want you to see this."

As she continued to gaze upward through the spiral staircase, David approached her from behind and looked up through the tower.

"Isn't that pure artwork," Claire stated.

"I see your point," he replied. David then lowered his head. He had not been this close to Claire. He could smell the fragrance of her long brown hair. Then, suddenly, Claire spun around him and started ascending the stairs.

"Come on," she called back to him.

Disappointed that she was no longer close, he paused for a moment as he attempted to put his emotions back in check.

"Are you scared?" she asked from above.

"No, I'm not scared," he answered back, grabbing the rail and taking multiple steps at a time to catch up with her.

"Be careful," she said, as he met her at the first window. "Look at this view, and it only gets better the higher we go," Claire said, already continuing her ascent.

At the top of the stairs, they came to a small door. Claire stopped and looking back at David, asked, "Are you ready for the grand prize—the lantern room?"

They climbed a ladder and entered the glass-enclosed room. Dragging her hand along the rail, Claire slowly walked around the massive lens.

"Do you know what this is?" she asked, circling the rail.

"I think I've learned that much; it's a lens."

Not really listening to his answer, she added, "This

is the heart of the lighthouse."

She then stopped and looked up, "It's over six feet tall."

He had to admit that it was impressive. Claire paused to admire its glass prisms capturing the sunlight.

"This is a second-order lens, just like the one at Stone Ridge," she continued. "Now, let's check out the view."

David followed her out to the gallery deck.

"And what a view this is," Claire said with a wide smile of approval.

David looked out over the sound with the horizon in the distance. He then turned his attention to Claire. He watched her, as her long hair spiraled in the wind. She smiled, as she attempted to capture the strands, until she gave up and let the wind take the strands. The sun reflected in her hazel eyes, and her face radiated a look of content. She looked down at her watch. "We better get going; it's almost eleven."

***

A moment after entering the museum, David and Claire heard someone call out, "Claire."

"Hi, Emerson, I hope you haven't been waiting long. We were checking out the tower," Claire responded.

"I can't blame you for that. She's a beaut."

"This is David."

"Hi, David," Emerson said, reaching out to shake his hand.

"I'm glad to finally meet you," David replied.

"Sounds like you have quite an adventure in front of you," Emerson said, leading them over to a second-order lens on display. The door of the large pedestal was open

146

to reveal the clockwork mechanism.

"Of course, Claire told you I've been to the Stone Ridge light and examined the works?"

"Yes," David replied.

Emerson reached for a cardboard box sitting on the floor next to the lens. "Here are the parts you'll need." He opened the box to reveal a crank, a gear, and some screws.

"The clockwork seems in surprisingly good shape for not getting much attention over the years; it just needs a little oil. What worries me though is the rotation mechanism. I couldn't get in there to check the ball bearings."

"I guess that's a chance we have to take," David replied.

"Come on in here, and I'll show you what you're going to have to do."

David followed Emerson into the pedestal area.

"I'm afraid there isn't much room in here," Emerson said to Claire.

"That's fine. I'll amuse myself."

As the men were going over the details of the repair, Claire went through the museum, reviewing the displays. She examined the fourth- and fifth-order lenses and other artifacts, this time reading through the display descriptions, something she seemed to never have time to do.

A number of museum visitors were now collecting around David and Emerson. They were interested in the one-on-one instruction taking place. Emerson had to pause at times to answer questions from the group. David chuckled to himself, as this went on.

"And that's what the keepers had to do back in those days to keep the mechanism running," Emerson said, in an attempt to disperse the crowd.

Claire noticed the men were again alone, so she went back to join them.

"Now, we need to talk about the light," Emerson began. I was thinking you could just get a hold of a regular lantern, something at a camping store, but Claire tells me this light needs a distance of eighteen nautical miles. I think we really should use a genuine second-order lamp. Don't you have one of those on display at Stone Ridge?" he asked Claire.

"Yes, we do; it's the old standby lamp, but the mantel is missing."

"I have one of those in my car—brought it just in case. Now, as you probably already know, Claire, you have to make sure the lamp is sitting in the center of the lens."

"Yes," Claire responded.

"Once you get it all set up, you will want to crank the clock mechanism. This will have to be repeated about every two hours to keep it rotating. The characteristics for that light are six white flashes every ten seconds."

"That's right," Claire acknowledged.

"Looks like you two are in business. You have my cell number if you have any questions. When do you plan to do this?"

"The weekend before the anniversary. Wish we could start earlier, but this is the only time the place is closed for more than a day. It's the Blessing of the Fleet weekend," David answered.

"You're cutting it close. I'll make sure I keep my cell with me in case you need to call. Come with me to my car, and I'll get the wicks and mantel for you."

Once at his car, Emerson retrieved the lantern parts from his trunk.

"I'm planning on being in Stuart Cove on the fifth, can I pick up the crank then? Does that give you enough time?" Emerson asked.

"That's fine," David responded. "We only have one shot at this, and that's on the first."

Emerson began to drive out of the parking lot, but then stopped and backed up to reach David and Claire. Leaning out of his window, he said, "I almost forgot; you need to pick up some kerosene for the lantern."

"Geez," Claire responded. "I almost forgot that. Thanks, Emerson."

Keeping to David's promise, they stopped by the grocery store to pick up the fixings for a steak dinner.

"When was the last time you used that grill?" David asked, joining Claire in the kitchen.

"I don't think it was that long ago. Why do you ask?"

"Because I noticed it was full of cobwebs."

Claire laughed, "Well, I guess it's been longer than I thought."

While Claire was cutting up a carrot for the salad, David reached around and grabbed a small piece that had fallen off the cutting board. As he did this, his hand brushed up again her arm. He felt the warmth of her skin and hesitated. She immediately drew back and went to the refrigerator to gather the lettuce. Noticing her discomfort, David decided not to acknowledge what had just happened.

"How do you like your steak?" he asked.

"Medium rare," Claire called back, still collecting salad items from the refrigerator. David left to tend the grill.

It was early evening by this time, and a light breeze blew through the branches of the large cedar tree standing in the backyard. The position of the house on the property offered a false sense of seclusion and a feeling of privacy in the backyard.

"What's this?" Claire asked, opening the rear screen door.

"I thought we'd take advantage of the lovely evening and eat out here." David had moved the table and chairs sitting up against the house to an area under the cedar tree. Sitting on the now clean table was a beer glass full of random wildflowers freshly picked from the field next to the house.

"I guess I can't turn down this offer. I'll bring the salad out here."

"Let me help you with that," he responded.

***

"Now, I know why you consider that your specialty dish. That was probably the best grilled steak I've had," Claire said, sitting back in her chair, showing her satisfaction with dinner.

"And you doubted me," he replied.

"Well, I must say you didn't sound very convincing."

He refilled their wine glasses.

"David, we have to talk."

"I thought we were," he replied.

"You plan to be here in Stuart Cove until the fourth, right?"

"Yea, so I can be back to work on the seventh."

"I don't want to assume anything. I just want to be clear in case there's any question."

David suddenly knew where this conversation was going.

"We have to make sure we remain friends and nothing more."

So, her reaction earlier was not my imagination, David thought.

"Do we have an understanding?" she asked.

"Yes, we do," David answered. He raised his glass for a toast, but inside he felt unexpectedly empty. She returned the toast.

***

David was at the hardware store, picking up a new hinge for the closet door when he felt his cell phone go off.

"Hi, Claire," David said, seeing the call was from her.

"The radio is gone," Claire said with panic in her voice.

"Gone, what do you mean gone?" David responded, trying to control his reaction.

"I went into the office to get the other log, and I noticed it was not there. I went and asked Jim where it was, and he told me it was sold to a guy who collects old radios."

"Shit, we need that radio, Claire. We need to get it back. Find out who this guy is that they sold it to."

"Okay, I'll try. I just hope they tell me."

"We don't want all our work to be wasted," David responded. "Give me a call back as soon as you know something."

"I will."

Claire hung up the phone and walked around the grounds while she planned how she would word her inquiry. She did not want to raise suspicion by coming across as desperate, thereby causing them not to give her the information.

"Claire," Millie yelled from the backdoor of the keeper's house, "you have a group ready for a tour."

"I'll be right there," Claire yelled back. "Damn,"

she said to herself, as she headed back to the house.

"Hello, folks, you ready for a tour?" Claire asked, taking control of her external composure, while inside her anxiety mounted.

After completing the tour, Claire approached Millie who was working the cash register in the gift shop. "Millie, I understand that old radio that was in the lighthouse was sold to a collector."

"Yes, a gentleman bought it yesterday. He had an English accent," Millie responded.

"I know someone else who has an old radio they're looking to get rid of. Maybe this guy would like to buy that one as well. Do you know the man's name who bought it?"

"No, but maybe it's in this file. Let me look." Millie pulled a small plastic box up on the countertop and began looking through it.

Thank goodness, Claire thought.

"Yes, here it is—a Mr. Oliver Barnes. I'll write his phone number down for you."

"Thanks, Millie, and my friend thanks you."

"Looks like we have another group coming in," Millie said, handing Claire the piece of paper as she looked over Claire's shoulder and out the front window.

As soon as Claire was able to slip away, she called David. "I've got his name and number."

"Great," David responded. "Do you know how much he paid for it?"

"No, I didn't get that information, and I don't think I should go back and ask."

"That's fine. What is it? I'm going to give him a call right now."

Claire gave him the information and asked, "Do you think we have a chance of getting it back?"

"I sure to hell hope so," David responded, grateful

they got the information but uncertain as to whether they would actually get the radio back.

"Hello, is this Mr. Barnes?" David asked.

"Yes, it is, who's this?"

"My name is David Parker. I understand you bought an old radio from the Stone Ridge Lighthouse."

"Yes, I did, and if you're calling to get it back, might I remind you I bought it fair and square?"

"Mr. Barnes, I'm not from the lighthouse. I'm calling to say I'm interested in buying it from you."

"It's not for sale, Mr.—what did you say your name was?"

"It's David, and I'm willing to pay you twice what you bought it for," David said, sensing the conversation was not going, as he had hoped.

"David, I said it's not for sale. Now, I must be running along, I have to pick up my granddaughter at the airport."

"Mr. Barnes, please let me give you my phone number in case you change your mind."

"I'm telling you …."

David broke in, "Please, Mr. Barnes, can you take my number, just in case?"

"Well, all right, young man, but I have no plans to call you."

As David hung up, he felt exasperated. *All that we have gone through, the many hours of research, was it for nothing?* he thought. *No, I've invested too much to let this jeopardize our plans. I have to think of a way to resolve this setback.*

Arriving home from the lighthouse that evening, Claire immediately noticed there was something different, as she pulled in her driveway. For a moment, she could not identify what it was. She found David at the computer in the living room when she walked in.

153

"You trimmed those bushes in front of the house, didn't you?"

"Yea, I hope you don't mind, but it was driving me crazy. I found some clippers in the shed, so I thought I'd just take care of it."

"It looks nice, actually. Thanks."

Anxious to know, she asked, "So, did you call him?"

"Yes, and he is a very stubborn man. He won't sell it to me, not even for twice what he paid."

"What are we going to do then?" Claire asked, as she dropped into the overstuffed chair.

"As I see it, we don't have many choices; we give up, steal it, borrow it, or if I have any luck here, swap it."

"I don't like any of the choices, David. It's bad enough we're sneaking around the lighthouse, but stealing, that's another matter." She paused for a moment. "Did you say swap it?"

"Yea, I'm trying to find another one on the Internet that's for sale," David said, continuing his search.

"Wait a minute," she replied. "How are you going to swap it? Do you think he's going to go for that?"

"No, I don't think he will. That's the part I haven't figured out yet."

"This is not sounding good," Claire said, getting up and going in the kitchen.

David spent the rest of the evening searching and inquiring on the Internet. Claire decided to stay close by, so she lay down on the couch and read. It was half past eleven by the time David finally gave up. He noticed Claire had fallen asleep on the couch. He retrieved a blanket from her bed and covered her, and then went to bed.

The next morning, David's phone awakened him early.

"Hello," he said, trying to sound awake.

"Is this David?" the man on the other end of the phone asked.

"Yes, it is, what can I do for you?" David asked.

"You the guy looking for a channel receiver?"

Hearing this, David swung his feet over the side of the bed and sat straight up.

"Yes, it is, do you have one?"

"I know where to get one. I'm a dealer."

"Is it the exact model I'm looking for?" David asked.

"Sure is, I can have it for you next week."

"Next week won't do. I need it sooner than that." David suddenly realized he was coming across very belligerent and feared this might cause the man to delay it further. He decided he better change the course of the conversation.

"I just found out that my uncle has wanted that exact model for years, and his birthday is coming up, so I really wanted to surprise him."

"Well ..." The man paused. "I think I can get it today and send it rush delivery, but I'm going to have to charge you extra for that."

"I appreciate it, sir. It's real important to me," David responded.

David found Claire in the living room getting ready for work.

"I'm getting a channel receiver," he said to Claire.

"You are? Did you find one on the Internet?"

"I guess I did. A guy called me just now. Of course, I'm sure it helped that I put out a hefty offer. It should be here by Wednesday."

"Okay, so how are you going to solve the other part of the little problem? How the hell are you going to swap it with the other one, and besides, what if it looks different?"

"You have a lot of questions. I'm just trying to solve this one step at a time."

"I have to go to work now. You solve the problem and try to keep us from going to jail over this," Claire said, showing her irritation.

David stepped in front of her and put his hands on her shoulders. Looking into her eyes, he said, "Claire, you know I promised myself I would do what I could to accomplish what Danny was not able to, but I don't want to involve you if you don't want me to."

She began to relax under his touch. "I know you have devoted the last twelve months to this, and I know how much it means to you, but I'm getting a little scared."

David wrapped his arms around her and held her. "It'll be fine, Claire. I'll figure something out."

She suddenly felt safe and secure in his arms, but she knew she could not allow this emotion to take hold. She pulled back from David's embrace and gave him a friendly kiss on the cheek. "I have to get to work now."

***

"I don't think you're going to see an update from an hour ago," Claire said to David, as he sat at the computer, tracking the package on the Internet.

"Doesn't hurt to check," he replied.

"Have you figured out what you're going to do when you get it?"

"Yes, I think I have. I ..." Interrupting him, Claire held up her outstretched hand in protest. "Stop, don't tell me. I don't want to know."

"But ..." David tried to continue.

"That's all. Don't say any more. I'll see you tonight

after school." At that, she left David sitting at the computer with his mouth open, still trying to finish his sentence.

***

"I'm home," Claire said, walking in the house with her bookbag over one shoulder, inspecting the mail she had just collected from the mailbox. Without looking up, she threw her bookbag on the nearest chair. Then, once in the living room, she stopped and stared at the channel receiver sitting on the coffee table.

"Does it look like the one from the lighthouse?" David asked, as he entered the room, drying his hair with a towel.

Claire hesitated for a moment. She could not help but notice that David had just come out of the shower and was standing before her in only his jeans. Remembering their agreement, she suddenly collected her composure and sat on the couch. As she inspected the radio, she replied, "Actually, it looks better than the other one; it doesn't appear as old." Looking up at David, she said, "Now, I'm really worried. I was hoping you'd get an exact match."

"It'll be fine. I plan on doing the swap tomorrow."

Claire abruptly got up from the couch and went into the kitchen. From there, she yelled back, "I'm going to make a light dinner—soup and salad—you want some?"

"Sure, that sounds great; and don't worry, I won't tell you what my plan is for tomorrow."

"Good!" was the answer David received back from the kitchen.

David sat down in front of the radio and spent a few minutes inspecting his purchase. As he did this, he began to feel apprehensive about tomorrow's strategy. He knew he had to keep his feelings to himself, though, not to upset Claire. It was a relief when Claire called to say that dinner was ready.

"We're supposed to meet Kay and Dawson at Black Sand about five o'clock Saturday," Claire said, as they ate dinner.

"What about the lighthouse? When are we going there to do the repairs?"

"I arranged for us to be there at nine in the morning, but what if we don't get the radio back?" Claire asked.

"We have to assume I get that back, and we move on to the repairs."

"I didn't want to raise any suspicion, so I figured we'd meet with them at the park Saturday evening, go to the lighthouse afterward, and if you don't get it finished, we can go back there on Sunday."

"Raise suspicion? You're getting a bit paranoid, aren't you?" David asked. "If they don't see you, are they going to assume you are up to no good?" he continued with a chuckle.

"We'll probably need a break, anyway," Claire said, slightly embarrassed by his comment.

The next day proved very difficult for Claire at work. She began to have second thoughts about the plan David was about to carry out. She had never been involved in anything like this. Why, the worst thing she had done was take a box of candy from the drugstore by mistake when she was seven years old. She had been carrying it with her, as she followed her mother through the store. When they got to the cash register, she forgot it was in her hand. She did not notice it until they were in the car. Then, she was scared to say anything because she thought they might arrest her and her mother, so she kept it a secret. She could not even eat the candy; she hid it.

Her uneasiness did not go unnoticed by her co-workers.

"Geez, Claire, what's up with you? You seem awfully jumpy today," James, the department's lead analyst, commented.

"I seem jumpy to you?"

"Yes, you do."

"I don't know, maybe I didn't get enough sleep last night." As soon as she said this, she realized how bizarre it must have sounded.

"Didn't get enough sleep? Yea, I act like that, too, when I don't get enough sleep," James said mockingly with a grin on his face. Claire realized she needed to do a better job of hiding her anxiety, even though James was making light of it. She desperately wanted to call David to make sure he was okay, but she did not dare. As the day dragged on, she tried not to think about the awful things he could be going through. *He could get arrested or worse*, Claire thought. She tried to take her mind off it and concentrate on her work, but instead, she became angry at herself for letting him go through with it. Then, she found herself trying to justify why she did not stop him. *This was extremely important to him, and I don't want to be the one responsible for getting in the way.*

"Claire," Chery repeated for a second time before Claire looked up from the pile of paperwork on her desk.

"I'm sorry, I didn't see you there," Claire finally acknowledged.

"Yea, I noticed. I'm going to run over to the deli for lunch. You wanna join me?"

Claire looked down at the paperwork and hesitated.

"Come on, Claire, let's go."

"I guess this can wait," Claire responded. Grabbing her purse, she joined Chery, and the two left the office to walk to the nearby deli.

"So, what is going on with you, and don't give me

the same lame story you gave James about being tired?"

"That was pretty lame, wasn't it?" Claire said, as they walked across the street.

"Is it David?"

"No, why would you say that?" Claire said, scared that any mention of him would reveal his mission.

The local deli was especially popular for those working in the neighborhood, with lunch being the most crowded time. In addition to the inside dining, there were tables outside on the sidewalk. Two windows extended out on either side of the front entrance. The tables inside these windows were popular because of the view of the outside, especially in the colder months. It had the decor of a coffee house—dark-colored counters, chairs scattered throughout the premises, and a wicker basket containing the day's newspapers, with the pages no longer neatly in order.

As they entered the busy deli, they took their place in the food order line.

"Why don't you grab that empty table over there in the window while I get our order?" Chery said.

"I want a small Cobb salad with a decaf coffee. Here's a ten."

"That's all you're having?"

"Yea, I'm not real hungry."

As she took the ten from Claire, Chery sighed in reaction. When Chery approached the table a short time later, she found Claire staring out the front window, obviously deep in thought.

"Hello, Earth to Claire."

"I'm sorry," Claire responded, moving items out of the way, so Chery could place the tray on the table.

Sitting down, Chery said, "Look, Claire, you have to 'fess up. Something happened with David?"

Claire realized she had to say something. Chery was

not going to give up.

"Yea, I guess I am getting a little distracted thinking about David."

"Did something happen?" Chery asked, very interested to hear any romantic details that might be revealed.

"No, nothing happened, but I think I might be falling for this guy."

"Claire, let me tell you a secret—you fell for this guy a long time ago."

"No, I didn't. We've just been friends."

"Yea, okay, that's the way you see it, but that's not the way it looks from here, and besides, the guy is crazy about you."

"What makes you think that?" Claire asked, a little embarrassed by this comment.

"Oh, Claire, you are naive. I can see it in how he looks at you, can't you?"

The real answer was yes, Claire had noticed, but she had tried to disregard this notion. She did not want to get involved with someone who would be leaving soon—that was their agreement. Claire looked down at her lunch, but she was not very hungry. She just picked at it.

"He's leaving soon, so—well, we just have to stay friends." Claire struggled with this thought.

"He's still staying at your place, right?"

"Yea, why?"

"Just asking," Chery said, finishing her lunch.

At exactly five o'clock, Claire grabbed her things and headed out of the office. As she was leaving, James yelled out to her, "You better go home and get right to bed. Take care of those jitters." His laughter could be heard, as she went out the door.

She drove home as fast as she felt she could without risking the chance of getting pulled over. Since she was now alone, she allowed her feelings to fully take hold. The panic was affecting her judgment, though. She almost pulled out in front of someone as she was leaving a stop sign.

Get a hold of yourself, you fool, she thought. *You're going to get yourself killed if you're not careful.* She took a deep breath in an attempt to calm herself.

So, what the hell am I going to do if he's not there? Do I check the local police stations? Do I attempt to find out where Mr. Barnes lives? All this was running through Claire's mind as she approached her street. Seeing David's car in the driveway caused the panic to dissipate. Yet she felt that she needed to see him, to know he was all right. Claire hardly had the car in park before she jumped out and ran to the front door.

Bursting in, she found David sitting on the couch with what looked to be the lighthouse channel receiver sitting on the coffee table in front of him.

There was concern in her voice, "David."

"Yes," he calmly responded.

"You got it. You're all right. Everything went okay?" Claire could not get the words out fast enough.

David got up, took her hand, and led her over to the stuffed chair. "Calm down. Can I get you some water or something?"

"I'm fine," Claire responded. "What happened," she paused, "or do I want to know?"

"I'll tell you what happened if you let me," David said, going to get her a glass of water.

"Tell me."

David returned with the water. Handing it to Claire, he said, "I'm not real crazy about the fact it is so easy to find out where someone lives by checking the Internet, but in this case, it did come in handy. Turns out he's only about ten miles away from here."

"He's that close by?" Claire responded, feeling a little uneasy.

"I wasn't sure if he would be home during the day, so I just decided to drive over and check. I figured I'd do the swap while he was home."

"Are you crazy?" Claire interrupted.

"I figured that would be safer," he responded.

"Safer? How do you figure that?" Claire was getting more upset, as David continued recounting his experience.

"I parked in front of his house, figured I'd leave the other radio in the car, then I went up and knocked on his door."

Claire, at this point, just stared at David.

"After we exchanged a few words, he let me into his house. He's a very nice gentleman by the way." David hesitated.

"Go on," Claire said.

"Once he let me in, we talked in the living room for a little while. He told me how he had been interested in radios since he was a lad in England. He grew up in the small town of Lavenham, England."

"That's nice, but what about the radio?"

"I'm getting to that," David replied. "After we chatted, he took me to his study where his collection was located. There were about eight radios, including ours— quite a collection. Anyway, he went into the kitchen to get me something to drink. While he did that, I went out to the car and got the other radio, and then I swapped them." David stopped his story and sat back, quite satisfied with himself.

Claire, sitting there in amazement, asked, "How the hell did you do that without his seeing you?"

"I'm good, what can I say?" David responded, getting up from the couch to get a beer from the kitchen.

Claire followed him in. "How did he not see you or hear you?"

"All right, I'll come clean with you," David responded, turning to face her in the kitchen.

"Actually, I thought the story about my old uncle worked so well to get the other radio, I'd use it for this too. I told him that radio used to be my deceased uncle's, and it carried sentimental value for my aunt. If it wasn't going to be at the lighthouse, I wanted to get it back to my aunt, and in exchange, I would give him the other radio, same model and year, and it even worked. He went for it."

"That's what happened? You just went in there and talked him into it? Do you have any idea what I went through today worrying about you?" Claire said as she began to pound her fists against David's chest. "You really had me going."

David grabbed her wrists. "I tried to tell you what my plan was, but you wouldn't let me."

David was touched that Claire cared enough about him to worry all day. He had so far suppressed his feelings for her, but knowing that she had been thinking about him this way took him over the edge. As he tenderly held her wrists, he looked straight into her eyes, and she stopped and returned his gaze. They both knew their relationship was about to change. David gently kissed her on the lips. As Claire returned his affection, he put his arms around her, and placing his palms on the base of her back, he pulled her against him. The emotion that had been building between them was now released in a passionate kiss.

"I thought we agreed not to go here," Claire said softly in his ear, as he held her close.

David stopped and again looked into her eyes. "I know, but I want you, Claire. I can't keep denying that."

"I want you too," she said.

David responded with a deep amorous kiss. He then reached around and, slipping his arm behind her knees, lifted her up and took her back to his bedroom. She wrapped her arms around his neck, sensing the strength in his arms, as he carried her. She felt safe and secure. He gently placed her on his bed.

"Are you sure about this?" David asked, as he began kissing her neck.

"Yes," she responded.

***

The morning sun poured through the sheer curtains of the bedroom, causing Claire to slowly wake up. She could feel David next to her, and as she opened her eyes, she found him looking back at her.

"What are you doing?" she asked in a tone so quiet, he barely heard her.

"I'm admiring you."

"I must look awful."

"You're beautiful," David replied and put his arms around her to bring her close.

After a moment, Claire pulled away and ran into the bathroom. "I have to get to work. If I don't get out of here, I'm going to be late; you're a bad influence on me," she called back.

"I'll call your work and tell them you're sick, okay?" David yelled through the bathroom door.

"You better stay away from that phone," Claire called back.

Later, she found David in the kitchen making coffee. He had on only his jeans. Claire approached him from behind and reached her arms around him to stroke his chest.

"I wanted to do this the other day when I saw you come out from your shower."

David turned around to face Claire. "So, why didn't you?" he asked.

"Because we had an agreement." As Claire said this, she felt as if she was just snapped back to reality.

She turned away from him, got the coffee cups out of the cupboard, and placed them on the counter. David sensed what had just happened and turned Claire toward him again.

"Claire, do you think I'm just going to leave you?"

"You have to; you have a job and a home in New York."

"Don't you realize I've fallen in love with you, Claire?"

Claire put her arms around David. As she did this, he said in her ear, "We'll figure something out."

After a tender kiss on the lips, she turned back to the coffee cups. She trusted his sincerity but feared the actuality of the situation.

***

Miss Claire Reid, I do believe you're glowing," Chery said, approaching Claire's desk.

"Stop, you're going to make me blush."

"Come on; I've got our lunch. Let's eat in the break room."

They sat at an open table in the corner.

"So, come clean," Chery said, handing Claire her sandwich.

"What the hell happened? Yesterday, you were a bundle of nerves. Now, you look like …" Chery hesitated, then looking around to check if anyone was listening, leaned into Claire and asked, "Did you have sex with David?"

"Chery!" Claire said, as her cheeks began to flush.

"I knew it," Chery said.

"Do you mind?" Claire said with a smile of embarrassment.

"I could tell you guys were crazy about each other, and with him staying there at your place, I can put two and two together."

"But, Chery, it's complicated."

"What's complicated? Two young attractive adults get together," Chery said.

"He's going back to New York soon. He has a job and a home there."

"So, why don't you go with him?"

This thought had not entered Claire's mind until that moment.

"I can't do that."

"Why not?"

"For one, he hasn't asked me, and what the hell would I do in New York? I'm not a city girl," Claire responded.

"Do you love him?"

Claire put her sandwich down and sat up straight in her chair.

"Yes, I do," Claire responded with total confidence in her voice.

"So, if you love him, you will do what you have to to be with him."

"Maybe you're right, but this is exactly why I didn't want this to happen. Our lives are very different."

"Do you think you're the only one this has happened to? Other couples somehow work it out when the desire is there."

"I don't want him to make any changes in his life on my account," Claire said.

"Look, he's a big boy. He's fully capable of making decisions, and so are you. Believe me, if you just let things happen, it will work out one way or the other. By the way, that glow does look good on you."

"Stop that," Claire responded, hiding behind her sandwich.

***

The foot traffic in downtown Stuart Cove always increased during the weekends. This would begin during the day on Fridays. David had discovered the secret parking places around town, something only known by the locals. This Friday was turning out to be a pleasant late July day, temperature in the low 80s and clear skies. He thought back to the days when he first arrived at Stuart Cove to take care of his aunt's affairs; the feeling he had then about the town, as if he were seeing it for the first time. Similar feelings came back to him today, as he leisurely strolled up Main Street. He allowed himself to fully take in his surroundings—pausing to look into the display windows, watching the interactions of the locals, and observing their tranquil demeanor. He realized this time was different, though. Now, he was seeing everything from a new perspective.

Photographs of area homes partially covered the display window of the business. The sign hanging above the sidewalk read *Stuart Cove Realty*. As David reached out to grab the doorknob, the door opened. A fawn-colored greyhound, with her head held high, proceeded through the doorway. On the other end of the leash was her owner—a dark-haired woman in her forties.

"I'm sorry," the woman said.

David reached to pet the dog on the head. "She's beautiful. Is she a rescue?" he asked.

"Yes, she is."

"My parents had a greyhound when I was young; they're great dogs."

"They most certainly are," the woman replied.

David stood aside to allow them to exit, and then proceeded through the door.

"Mr. Parker is here to see you," the young blond receptionist said, leading David into Ellen's office.

"David, how nice to see you." She hesitated. "Did we have an appointment today I forgot about?"

"No, I thought I'd just pop in and see if you were here."

"That's fine. You worried me for a moment, though. Have a seat. What's up?"

"I need to talk to you about the cottage."

"Yes, since our meeting a few weeks ago, I have made progress getting the word out that it will soon become available for rent. I have met with some of my associates. We ..."

David interrupted her. "Sorry to interrupt, Ellen, but my situation has changed. I don't want to rent it out."

"That's fine; we can change this to a sale if you like," she added.

"I don't want to sell it, either." A puzzled look came over Ellen. "I want to move into it."

Hearing this, a broad smile came over Ellen's face. She stood up, came around from behind her desk, and hugged him.

"Well, it looks as if I just lost a customer and gained a neighbor."

David did not expect this reaction. "Thank you," he said, a little embarrassed.

Leaning against the desk, Ellen asked, "So, what happened to cause this sudden change in plans? Does it have anything to do with Claire?"

169

David gave her an inquisitive look and began to say, "There are no secrets ..." Then, they said simultaneously, "... in this town."

Laughing, Ellen added, "I'm really glad to see you joining us."

"You know what, Ellen? Now that I have made my decision, I'm feeling very comfortable with it."

Once back on Main Street, he dialed Claire at work.

"This is Claire Reid, can I help you?" she said in a professional manner.

"Claire, it's David."

"Hi, David," she responded with recognition and a noticeable elation in her tone.

"I want you to meet me at the Ivy Inn for dinner tonight."

"The Ivy Inn? That place is fancy. Are you sure?" she asked, knowing it was way out of her budget range.

"Yes, I'm sure. I want to take you some place special tonight."

"Well, it looks like we have a date then," Claire said, delighted at the prospect.

"I'll make reservations for half past five then. Does that give you enough time?"

"Sure does. I guess I'll see you there."

A moment later, Chery came by Claire's desk to give her a copy of the report they were working on together.

"David's taking me to the Ivy Inn tonight," Claire said in a playfully vain manner.

"Oh, is he now?" Chery responded. "And what is the occasion?"

"Does there have to be an occasion? Maybe he just wants to take me to a nice place."

"Maybe," Chery said with a slight wink.

***

"David Parker," Claire stated to the maître d', assuming that would be the name he used for the reservation. Looking down at his paper, he responded, "Yes, this way, please." Claire followed him to the table where David was already seated.

"Hi, David," Claire said, taking the seat across from him, as it was offered by the maître d'.

"Good evening, Miss Reid," David replied.

"This is some place you selected," she said, glancing past David's shoulder to the large stone fireplace, where a painting of an early sailing vessel hung on the wall.

"It has a very good reputation," he replied.

"Can I start you off with drinks?" the tall slender server politely asked.

"I'd like to see your wine list," David said, and then pausing, he looked at Claire. "If that's all right with you."

"That's fine," Claire responded.

"Certainly, I'll bring that right away."

"The wine list?" Claire questioned. "A bottle for the two of us?"

"It's usually not very economical to order it by the glass, but don't feel like we have to finish off the bottle."

The server returned and handed David the wine list. As she did this, she explained, "Our specials this evening, starting with the appetizer, is the stuffed calamari, grilled and stuffed with lobster meat in a curry cream sauce drizzled with balsamic reduction sauce. Our entrées include the Atlantic salmon served over Creole bucatini pasta with garlic, olive oil, and fresh basil. We also have a grilled tilapia with Dijon mustard and smoked honey butter, and finally, the oven-roasted chicken breast stuffed with garlic herb cheese and served with lemon butter. I'll return shortly to get your order."

"Thank you," David said, looking over the wine list.

"Those all sound good," Claire commented, looking over her menu.

"Do you like calamari?" David asked.

"Yes, I love it," she responded, closing her menu.

The server returned a moment later, "Have you decided?"

"Yes, I think we have," David said and nodded to Claire.

"I'll take the tilapia special."

"And I'll have the salmon, but we'd like to start with the calamari you mentioned. We'll share that."

"Good," the server responded, making note of the order. "And your choice for a wine?" she continued.

"We'll take the '95 Droin Chardonnay, please."

"Very good choice, sir," the server responded, as she collected the menus.

"I guess this is our first real date," Claire said.

"I guess it is."

The wine steward then approached the table. He placed the glasses on the table and presented the wine bottle to David. "Sir, your 1995 Droin Chardonnay."

With a nod from David, the steward poured a small amount of the wine into David's glass and stood back waiting for approval.

"That's fine," David responded.

Watching this, Claire began to feel uncomfortable. She saw a side of David she had not seen before. He seemed quiet at ease in this environment. She thought about what his life was like in New York—the strict contrast it must be to Stuart Cove.

The steward then proceeded to pour the wine for Claire and then again for David, after which he placed the bottle in the chiller.

"I would like to propose a toast," David said, raising his glass.

"A toast?" Claire asked.

"Yes, I would like to toast to my decision to move to Stuart Cove."

Hearing this, Claire suddenly put her glass down, got up, and gave David a hug around his neck.

"Careful, honey," he said. "You're going to make me spill my wine."

Claire sat back down. Looking across at David, she was speechless for a moment.

"When did this happen? When did you decide this?" she asked.

"I've been thinking about it for a while, but I took the first step today. I met with Ellen and told her I would be moving into the cottage."

Claire got up again and gave David a kiss.

"What about our toast?" he said with a smile.

Claire sat down again, smiled back, and raised her glass for a toast.

"So, what about your job and your condo?" she asked after taking a sip of the wine.

"I've contacted a realtor in New York to start the process. I should make a bit of a profit, which I'll be able to live off until I work out a job in this area. I figure I'll give my notice in person when I go back next week."

Claire, feeling responsible for what seemed like a sudden life-changing decision, asked, "David, are you sure you'd be happy here? It's nothing like New York."

David could sense her concern. He put his glass down, leaned across the table, and said with an air of complete confidence, "Claire, you need not worry. This is something I have been thinking about since I first came back, and you, well, you're just icing on the decision cake.

She laughed, "I'm what?"

***

David woke up much earlier than usual this Saturday morning. Claire was still sleeping, as he lay there thinking about his decision to move to Stuart Cove. He was excited about the thought and did not feel any regret or, as he compared it to, *buyer's remorse.* He took that as a good omen— that he had made the right decision. He decided to quietly get up, make breakfast, and maybe even surprise Claire. Sam, who had been sleeping between them, looked a little confused seeing David get up first, but he soon determined that it really didn't matter who got up first, as long as the first one up fed him.

Claire came into the kitchen just as David was sliding the second omelet on the plate.

"What good timing," he said.

Claire, wearing her oversized tee shirt and rubbing her eyes, responded, "You made breakfast?"

"Why, yes, I did. I can make more than steaks on the grill. You awake? You look awful tired."

"I slept really well last night, I guess too well. I'm still tired."

"Maybe this will help wake you up," David said, handing her a mug of fresh coffee.

"Perfect, can you do this every morning?"

"No promises."

***

"Did you give them the story we're doing more research?" David asked, as they pulled up to the keeper's house.

"Yes, which is partially true. I'm going to do research while you're working on the light."

"Does that make you feel better, telling just half a lie?" David asked as they walked in and disarmed the alarm.

Claire turned back and gave him a playful smack on the shoulder.

"You should know me by now. I love to do the research, and this gives me some time to do that."

"Whatever you say, honey," David responded.

Carrying the box of parts Emerson provided, David took the lighthouse keys from Claire. "Since I have no idea how long this is going to take me, I better get started."

"That's fine. I'll meet you there later," she responded.

Claire decided she would check to make sure the lantern they would be borrowing Tuesday was still there.

They got rid of the radio at the most inappropriate time. Sure hope they don't try the same with the lantern, she thought.

There in the display case was the brass second-order lens lantern, beautifully polished. It looked like most oil lamps of the day but larger. It had a brass handle riveted to the body and a tall glass chimney. Claire examined it closely, wondering about the time it was last used. She knew it was sometime in 1932. She decided she would target her research to finding out more about the last keeper who lit the lantern. The thought of this and realizing that their plans were starting to come together, she found herself getting excited about the prospect of what they were going to do. She went back downstairs and retrieved a box from the parlor, which she took into the dining room and placed on the dining room table. She made herself comfortable and began to carefully examine the artifacts that had been stored and not yet sorted.

Later, looking at her watch, she found it was already half past ten. Seeing this, she thought about David and decided to check on his progress. As she stood up, she was startled to hear someone at the front door. She quickly walked toward the front foyer, hoping to see David, but instead her heart seemed to skip a beat when she saw Jim walking in.

"Jim, what are doing here?" Claire asked, trying not to sound as alarmed as she felt.

"Hey, Claire, I thought I'd take advantage of the place being closed and get some things done around here. Where's David? I thought he was here with you."

"He's in the lighthouse, looking at some things. I've been looking through papers here in the dining room. I found some interesting things. Can I show you?" Claire's mind was racing. This was all she could come up with for the moment, but she figured that if she could get Jim distracted, she could somehow warn David.

"Sorry, not right now, I really want to get started," he said, continuing down the hall toward the backdoor.

"Where are you going?" Claire asked, realizing he was headed for the lighthouse.

"I'm going to the light; is everything all right? You sound upset."

"I'm fine. I just wanted to know where everyone was."

As soon as Jim went out the backdoor, Claire called David on his cell phone.

"Answer, damn it," she said aloud, as each ring went unanswered. She then quickly hung up and ran to the lighthouse, not knowing what she would do, but deciding she'd figure it out when she got there.

Rushing through the door, she found Jim on his way up the tower.

"Jim," Claire yelled, much louder than she needed to for him to hear her.

He stopped and looked down the stairs at her, "What, Claire? Why are you shouting?"

"I wanted to know if you'd like a soda. I was going to bring one to David." She continued to say this in a loud voice in an attempt to warn David of the visitor.

"No, I'm fine," he said and continued his ascent up the stairs.

Claire realized she had done all she could. Now, she had to hope it worked.

"Hey, David," Jim said, entering the small office.

"Hi, Jim, come to join us in our research?" David responded in a calm voice.

"No, afraid not, I have other work I should be getting done. What the hell's wrong with Claire? She's acting pretty strange."

Claire then appeared in the doorway, a bit out of breath.

"I thought you were bringing David a soda. What d'ya forget it?"

Claire, looking straight at David, realized he must have had enough warning to put everything away.

"Yea, I guess I did."

"I think this girl is wacky," Jim said jokingly, leaving to go up to the lantern room.

As soon as he left the room, Claire turned to David, "Why didn't you answer your phone?"

"I was too busy putting things away. I saw his car when he drove up. You need to calm down," he said and put his arm around her. "You're going to make him suspicious."

"I know, but I was scared. I didn't know what to do," she replied.

"It's okay. We're fine," David said, and then kissed her.

"So, how far did you get? It looks as if Jim is going to be here for a while."

"I actually got it working, but I don't like the sound of it. I'm worried about the bearings. I know we can't change them, but I'm going to have to at least lubricate the bearing assembly. We can come back tomorrow, can't we?"

"Yes, I already worked that out," she answered.

***

Claire and David arrived at the park to find a larger crowd than the previous year.

"There's Sean and Larry," Claire said, waving her hand to get their attention.

"I'm not real crazy about that guy, Larry," David said to Claire, as they headed in their direction.

"He's fine," she responded.

"Hey, you two just get here?" Sean asked.

"Sure did," David answered.

Sean, noticing they were holding hands, commented, "So, you guys are an item, I see."

Claire, smiling back, replied, "I guess you could say that."

"You ever write that story about the *Seahawk*?" Larry interrupted.

David, already annoyed by his question, but not wanting to upset Claire, answered, "Not yet."

"I thought you'd be done by now," Larry said.

Claire, sensing David's irritation, squeezed his hand and replied instead. "That's not the only story he's been

working on, Larry. He'll do it when he has the time."
Then changing the subject, she added, "So, where's the
rest of the gang?"

Larry, who was impervious to David's reaction to
him, responded, "Chery and Dawson are over at the first
pavilion."

"Great, I think we'll go say hi to them," Claire said
and quickly pulled David along.

"I still think he's a jerk," David said, as they headed
for the pavilion.

"Sorry about that. Guess he doesn't know when to
keep his mouth shut."

"I'll do it for him, if he doesn't watch it."

Chery and Dawson were busy helping get the food
ready when Chery looked up to see David and Claire
approaching them.

"Claire, you made it." Then, turning her attention to
David, she added, "So, you finally had the sense to make
a move on Claire."

Hearing this, Claire became embarrassed. "Chery,
do you mind?"

Chery, not acknowledging Claire, continued, "So, I
understand you took her to the Ivy Inn last night."

"Chery!" Claire said, still attempting to stop the
conversation.

"Yes, I did," David replied, amused by the
attention.

"So, what was the occasion?"

"Chery, I want you to stop talking, do you hear
me?" Claire said, as she now tried to put her hand over
Chery's mouth.

"I told her I would be moving to Stuart Cove."

"I knew it," Chery yelled out, as she playfully
grabbed Claire's wrists, so Claire could not cover her
mouth.

"The way news travels around this town, I'm surprised you didn't know already," David said in amusement.

"Everyone will know now," Claire said.

"Are you trying to say I am the source of the information around here?" Chery asked, now turning her attention to Claire.

"Just stating facts," Claire said teasingly.

"Looks like the main course is being served, ladies," David broke in, sensing the timing was right.

After partaking in the feast, Claire and David decided to take a walk.

"I want to take you to the area where Danny and I went while he was telling me his story."

Intrigued, Claire agreed. By this time, it was early evening, and the sun had begun its descent, turning the sky light orange across the horizon. Along the shoreline, the slight waves thrust the churning surf to claim the sand, only to pull back and relinquish it once again. Claire removed her sandals to feel the cool sand on her bare feet. They walked slowly hand-in-hand, enjoying the cool breeze and the colors of the sunset. They did not speak as they passed another couple huddled close together on the sand and a young woman with her black lab. They stopped a moment to watch the woman, as she held the large stick in her hand. The lab, dripping wet, stared intensely at the stick, waiting for it to move. Then, the women reached back and threw it out in the water. The dog immediately ran out, pouncing through the small waves, and then swam out toward the stick. David and Claire smiled at each other in response to this performance and continued their walk. As they approached the narrow area of the beach, the nearby trees swayed against the breeze.

"I think this is it," David said, finding sea-dried

trees scattered throughout the area. David took Claire by the hand and guided her to sit next to him in the sand against a dried tree trunk. He put his arm around her, as they looked out over the water.

"This is a nice spot," Claire commented.

"This is where Danny told me about the storm."

They both sat in silence for a moment.

"I'm scared, Claire. I'm scared I might let him down."

Claire squeezed his hand to show her support but felt it best she not reply, rather to listen, and allow David to express his concerns.

"Danny shared with me what he apparently had not shared with anyone else. He risked the fact that I might think him a fool. I'm sure he knew of the rumors. He trusted me with the truth, and I still don't know why. Maybe he somehow knew something about me that I didn't. Doesn't that sound weird?"

"No, you might be right," Claire responded.

"But how, how would he know? I can't explain that, and I can't explain that radio. All I know is that meeting this guy Danny changed my life, and I've been driven by this quest ever since."

David paused. "I don't even know what to expect if we get the light back on." Again, he paused. "Claire," he said, "what if we can't get the light back on? What if the call doesn't come in?"

Claire looked into David eyes. "What did Danny tell you —*everything happens for a reason*? Whatever happens, it'll be okay."

David kissed her and then whispered into her ear, "I hope you're right."

***

Claire saw to it that David would not be late for the church service the next morning. She set the alarm and made sure she allowed enough time to cook them a good breakfast.

"Have you seen the grease I picked up at the hardware store?" David asked, wandering around the house, looking in odd places.

"Did you look on the desk?" Claire responded.

"Ah, no, I didn't look there. I'd like to go straight to the lighthouse after the service."

"That's fine," Claire said, placing the plates on the counter bar.

After a moment, Claire stated, "You know I'm a bit uncomfortable about not getting permission for Tuesday night."

"It'll be fine. If they find out we were there, you just tell them we had to go by and pick something up for our research and that you figured they wouldn't have a problem with that. I really don't want to take the chance of asking permission and possibly getting turned down because then, you really would get in trouble."

"I guess you're right," Claire responded, finishing her breakfast.

As Claire and David entered the church, they noticed it was filling up quickly. They found a couple of empty spots in the pew next to Mr. and Mrs. Beardsley, an elderly couple from town.

"Good morning," Mrs. Beardsley said, as they sat down.

"Good morning," Claire responded.

Mr. Beardsley leaned forward to talk around his wife, "This place is always bursting at its seams during Christmas, Easter, and the Blessing of the Fleet. I don't know how we fit everyone in."

"Yes, I see what you mean," David said, as he

noticed men bringing folding chairs to the rear of the church.

Whispering in David's ear, Claire said, "There's Cynthia."

David nodded his head, as he spotted her sitting in the same area she had the year before. *I hope I don't let your father down*, David thought.

***

David and Claire turned down the invitation they received from their friends for brunch at the diner. Instead, they went straight to the lighthouse.

"Will it bother you if I continue my research in the office?" Claire asked, organizing the paperwork she had gone over the day before and placing it back in the box.

"No, I've finished the difficult part of the repairs, or at least, I hope I have. Let me get that," David said, taking the box from Claire. They left the dining room and proceeded to the lighthouse. On the way there, Claire asked, "What if Jim shows up again?"

"You're going to have to figure out how to distract him for a while—keep him away from the office."

"That might not be easy to do," Claire responded, as they made their way up the spiral staircase.

Entering the room, David placed the box on the desk. He then turned his attention to the lens pedestal. Opening the panel, he said, "I have to make some minor adjustments and then add some grease to the rotation mechanism. Just hope my handiwork holds up."

"I'll stay out of your way."

Claire extracted the information from the box that she had sorted the day before. Carefully laying it out on the desk, she spent time going through it.

"His name was Ross Hunter," Claire finally said,

183

breaking the silence.

"Who are you talking about?" David asked.

"The last keeper who used that lantern. He was the keeper from 1922 to 1933. He had a wife, Ella, and two young girls, Lucilla and Betsy."

"You're pretty good at that research stuff," David said, taking a moment from his work to listen to Claire's discovery. He enjoyed watching her enthusiasm.

"I thought we should know who we were borrowing it from. I'll have to make sure we put that on the display card; it'll personalize it more."

David could not help but notice a powerful emotion come over him; it seemed to come from nowhere. He realized he was right where he wanted to be in his life, sharing a moment with the person he wanted to be with. The strong professional aspirations he once held were suddenly replaced, and he felt completely at peace with his decision to leave that past life. He felt happy, genuinely happy. He smiled to himself and said, "I think we're ready for a test drive."

Standing back to admire his work, he added, "Where's the crank?"

Claire found the box they had tucked away from the day before. "Here it is."

"You ready for this?" David asked.

"I'm nervous," she replied.

David connected the crank and began turning it.

"It's working," Claire yelled, exhilaration in her voice.

David stood back, put his hands on her hips, and smiled.

"I think we did it, Claire. I think we're in business."

Claire threw her arms around his neck. As she did this, David put his arms around her and brought her in close for a passionate kiss, as the large assembly rotated after being still for forty-four years.

***

Claire woke up in the dark and realized David was not next to her. She looked at the clock on the bedside table and noticed it was two a.m. Concerned, she got up and began searching the house. Choosing to keep the main lights off, she was guided by the nightlights located in various parts of the house. As she walked into the living room, she noticed Sam sitting in front of the open backdoor.

"Is David out there, Sam?" she asked. He got up and moved, as she approached the screen door. Looking out through the screen, she strained to see into the moonlit backyard. Once her eyes adjusted, she could see David sitting on the metal chair in the night shadow of the cedar tree. Feeling a desire to comfort him, she pushed open the screen door. Not wanting it to slam behind her, she gently controlled its closure.

David looked up to see Claire in her extra large pink t-shirt coming toward him. A slight breeze blew her long hair behind her. She stopped in front of him, and he placed his hands on her waist and looked up at her.

"Tomorrow is the first, you know," he said softly.

"Actually, it is tomorrow; it's two in the morning," she replied with a slight smile.

"I'm sorry, did I wake you?"

"Your absence woke me."

"I've been thinking a lot about Danny lately, going over his story, piece by piece, in my mind."

Claire gently brushed his dark hair across his

forehead.

"He didn't deserve the treatment he got. He was no crazier than we are."

"That might not be saying much," Claire said, smiling down at him. "What do you think is going to happen when we turn the light back on?"

"According to the ghost hunter, we'll be appeasing the spirits."

"And how do we know it's worked?" she asked.

"I'm not sure, but I know I have to get the light back on and write his story."

Claire placed her palms on either side of David's head. Tilting it back, she looked into his eyes, "And that's what we'll do."

Then, she leaned over and gently kissed him on the lips.

"Would you like to come to bed with me?" Claire asked.

"Yes, I think I would."

Claire took David's hand and led him to her bedroom.

***

They're still calling for storms tonight," Claire said, as David joined her in the kitchen.

"That shouldn't make a difference, but I'll be worried if we have any trouble with that lantern."

As David reached for the cup of coffee Claire was handing him, he realized she was not letting go.

"What are we going to do if we have trouble with the lantern?" she said, holding on to the cup.

"I bought a backup lantern," he replied, looking puzzled. "Can I have my coffee?"

"Oh, sorry. When did you get that?" she asked.

"I must have forgotten to tell you. I talked to Emerson the other day, told him how I was getting along with the repairs, and he suggested I buy a regular lantern as a backup."

"No, you didn't tell me that. Good thinking," she replied, as she got ready to go to work.

"Are you taking tomorrow off?"

"Yup, I'd rather not have to drag myself in to work after being at the light half the night."

"Excellent," he said, then kissed her goodbye.

David decided to take his coffee out to the backyard and enjoy the beautiful morning. Sitting under the cedar tree, he noticed a wren hopping around the grill—its tail straight up, bobbing its head as it moved about, chattering with curiosity. Out of the corner of his eye, he noticed someone else observing this performance. There at the screen door was Sam, his attention fixed on the little bird. David continued to watch Sam watch the bird, until the little wren, satisfied it had examined the grill thoroughly, flew away.

"You wanted a piece of him, didn't you, Samie?" he said, patting Sam on the head as he entered the house. Sam followed David to the kitchen. Then, stopping at one of the barstools, he decided to jump up to his perch where he could keep an eye on David, as he went about cleaning the dishes.

After spending the rest of the morning mowing the grass and taking care of other neglected yard chores, David went into town to finalize matters on the cottage and pay a visit to the local newspaper establishment. It was mid-afternoon by the time he was done. Not particularly in a hurry, he stopped at the pier and watched a fishing boat come in to unload its catch.

Her name was *Sandra*. She pulled up alongside the pier. A thin man with a beard, dressed in a tee shirt, dark brown oilers, and wearing a pair of thick rubber gloves began handing totes filled with ice and fish up to the men on the docks. These men took the totes into the fishery to be weighed and placed in boxes. As this activity played out, a single seagull landed on the net reel, picking what it could from the net. Other gulls noticed this, in the hope that a missed treasure of fish had been found. As they attempted to land on the reel, the first gull quickly fought them off, rightfully claiming its possession. The men continued their routine, handing off the totes, hosing off the dock, and boxing the fish.

David had begun to understand the hard work involved in this profession. He had respect for these men who chose this life, often because of a family tradition, and because it was in their blood. That was not the case for Danny, though. He had done it, carrying the guilt of Scott's loss. As David turned to leave, he found himself roughly eye-to-eye with a seagull sitting on a piling. The gull watched him, but did not leave his post. "Come here often?" David asked aloud. He received no response, only a concentrated stare as he passed by.

***

"Let's go," David said, tension in his voice. "The wind's really kickin' in."

"Has it started raining yet? Claire asked, rushing around the kitchen.

"I don't think so," he replied.

"I want to bring some snacks. We might be there for a while."

"Snacks? How can you think about eating? I don't know about you, but my stomach's in knots," David said.

They arrived at the lighthouse at 8:50. Already blanketed by darkness, the wind was noticeably stronger at the station. A light rain began to fall as they ran from the car to the house. After disabling the alarm, they both went upstairs to collect the lantern.

"There she is," Claire said, as she opened the back panel of the display case. After carefully removing it, she placed it on top of the case.

"Keeper Hunter, we ask your permission to borrow this lantern."

"What are you doing?" David asked.

"We know there are spirits out there on the water. We better make sure we appease whatever spirits might be here as well."

"You might have a point."

After Claire finished her request, David took the lantern, and they headed back downstairs.

"Here, let's put the lantern in this box with the other stuff. Can you carry that while I carry the radio?"

"I think I can handle it," Claire responded.

When they approached the backdoor, they realized the rain was now a downpour.

"Hold on, I'll get a couple of the raincoats to put over this stuff. We don't want it getting soaked," she said.

Claire came back with two yellow raincoats. She then wrapped them around the radio and the box.

"Any raincoats for us?"

"No, I'm afraid not."

"Then let's make a run for it," David said, as they left the house and headed for the tower.

Balancing the box on her knee, Claire had to fumble with the keys to get the door unlocked.

"Careful," he said, "don't drop it."

Once inside, they unwrapped the radio and the box from the raincoats and dried off using towels Claire had retrieved from behind the counter.

"Come on, let's get this stuff up there," David said, gathering the radio in his arms.

Once in the office, David placed the radio on the table where it had previously sat.

"There," David said, standing back, contemplating its exact position.

"Now, for the lantern."

Claire carefully took the lamp from the box and began cleaning the old mechanism.

"While you do that, I need to remove the light bulb assembly, so we have a place to put the lamp," David said, going up to the lantern room.

Claire continued working on the lamp, installing the mantel and removing the cap of the old fuel reservoir so that they could add the kerosene.

"It's been sixty-eight years since you've cast your light," Claire said to herself.

Carefully carrying it up to the lantern room, Claire was alarmed by the force of the rain against the glass and the sound of the wind swirling around the enclosure. Collecting herself, she called out loudly, "She's ready."

"I'm almost done," David called back. Then, after a moment, "Hand it to me."

"Be sure you center it in the lens."

"What?"

"Put it in the center of the lens," Claire yelled back.

"Like that?" David asked, waiting for approval.

"Perfect," she called back. "What time is it?"

"It's half past nine."

"When are we going to turn it on?" she asked.

"I don't want to take a chance of drawing attention to this place. We better wait until 9:45."

"Come on; let's go to the office. It's difficult to hear in here," David said, still yelling.

"I wonder if the storm tonight is at all like the night

they lost the *Seahawk*," Claire asked.

"It was much worse then, at least how Danny described it, but this does give us a hint of that night, I suppose."

Suddenly, there was a crack of thunder, and the lights flickered.

"Good thing we're not relying on electricity for this," David said as a lightning flash lit up the window.

"You're right, and we often lose the electricity here during storms. You better get the flashlight out of the drawer of that desk."

They sat listening to the storm, as it took hold around them, now sending the rain horizontally against the window.

"Does this mean we have a lighthouse ghost?" Claire asked.

"Maybe we do."

"Many lighthouses have resident ghosts, you know," Claire said, as the lights again flickered. "The Sentinel does," she continued. "The story goes that in 1855, a keeper there fell to his death, as he was carrying buckets of oil up the stairs. After the incident, there were reports of hearing footsteps walking up and down the staircase, even to this day."

"If you had asked me last year if I believed in such a thing, I would have laughed at you. Now, I'm not so sure," David said, looking at his watch.

"The Piney Point light is also haunted," Claire went on. "They say that the keeper there left on his boat to get their monthly supplies, but on his way back, a storm hit, and he never arrived. His wife, who was keeping the light lit during his absence, was incoherent when they finally got out to the light. She was obsessed with the light, and they had to drag her away to a mental hospital. Following that, there were many reports over the years of seeing a woman pacing the widow's walk when nobody was there. Boats in the area have reported hearing screams of a woman coming from the lighthouse."

Another crack of thunder, and the lights went out. Claire stood up and screamed.

"Are you all right?" David asked, turning on the flashlight and going over to comfort her.

"Yes, I'm fine. I just got scared. I must be crazy telling ghost stories during a storm, while we're waiting for a ghost to contact us."

David laughed and gave her a tender hug, "Yea, probably not the best idea."

"I guess we have to get to work," Claire said, attempting to collect herself.

"Let's get that lantern lit," David said, already heading up the stairs.

Reaching into his pocket, he brought out a lighter and proceeded to light the mantel. The flame caught hold, casting a brilliant blue. Then, after a moment, the room filled with light.

"It's beautiful," Claire said, admiring the brightness.

David went down and opened the pedestal, inserted the old crank, and proceeded to wind the clockwork. Then, as it did back before 1956, the lighthouse cast its light far out over the water, through the storm.

Claire came rushing down the steps and met David, as he backed out of the pedestal. "We did it," she screamed.

David lifted her off the ground, as he hugged her, then he quickly put her down and pointed the flashlight to his wrist.

"It's ten o'clock—the radio."

They both grabbed the chairs and pulled them close to the receiver.

"I'm both excited and scared," Claire said, looking at David.

"Actually, I am too. I know what I heard a year ago, but after this much time, it kinda feels as if it must have been a dream."

"I guess we'll find out," Claire responded.

They watched the radio, as the storm continued its relentless assault outside, and the rotation of the light cast its shadows throughout the room.

"Did it just get cold in here?" David asked.

"Yes, I think it did," Claire responded, as she crossed her arms and began to rub them with her hands in an attempt to warm up.

The radio began to crackle. Claire screamed, and David quickly put his palm across her mouth.

"Mayday—mayday—mayday—mayday— mayday—mayday, this is the fishing vessel *Seahawk,* our coordinates ...."

Static interrupted the call.

"... we are taking on water ..." More static. "... need help."

Then, the radio went quiet.

"YES!" David screamed.

Claire sat motionless, staring at the radio. A moment later, the lights came back on.

"Claire," David asked, still ecstatic about the call, "are you all right?"

"I expected it, but I didn't expect it," she said, still in shock.

With the lights back on, David could see how pale she was.

"I'm sorry, honey, I didn't consider how this would affect you. I wanted it so bad, to both prove I wasn't crazy and to hopefully, somehow, help Danny."

"That's all right. I wanted it too," Claire said, as she

pulled herself together.

"How long are we going to leave the light on?" she asked.

"I really don't know, but if we leave it on much longer, I'm afraid this place is going to be surrounded by cops. Let's give it another twenty minutes."

After they waited, David went upstairs to extinguish the light. As he did this, Claire went over to the radio and grabbed the cord. Finding the end, she confirmed to herself it was not plugged in.

"Do you feel better now?" Claire asked, as they drove home from the lighthouse.

"I'm not sure. We did what we set out to do."

"I think Danny would have been proud of you," she said.

"Maybe, but I still feel a void; something is missing."

"The story—you have to write his story. That's what's missing," she replied.

"Maybe you're right."

They continued their ride back to the house in the rain.

Chapter Eleven

The ringing of Claire's phone woke them both the next morning.

"Hello," Claire answered. Judging from the dim light shining through the window, she knew it was very early.

"Claire, it's Jim. Is David there?"

"Yes, he's here. Hold on."

Holding her hand over the receiver, Claire whispered, "David, it's for you. It's Jim from the lighthouse." She sat up. Distressed, she asked, "What do you think he wants? Did we leave something there?"

"Calm down. Hand me the phone, and I'll find out."

Claire handed David the phone.

"Hi, Jim, what's up?"

"Are you still doing that story about the *Seahawk*?"

"Yea, why do you ask?" David said, wondering why Jim would call so early in the morning to ask this question.

"I think you better get down here. I'm at the lighthouse."

This got David's full attention. "What's wrong, Jim? What's going on?"

"I'd rather tell you when you get here, and hurry up."

David hung up the phone and began getting dressed.

"What happened? What'd he say?"

"He just asked me if I was still writing about the *Seahawk*; said I should get over there right away." As he said this, David was grabbing a shirt from the drawer.

"I'm coming too," Claire said, quickly putting on a pair of jeans.

"Then hurry up."

The morning brought in a dense fog, slowly being disbursed by the early morning sun.

"This fog's going to slow us down," David said, as they got into his car.

The roads were still wet from the night before. Water propelled upward about the car, as they drove through the vast puddles.

"So, do you think we're in trouble?" Claire finally asked.

"No. If that were the case, Jim would have spoken to you rather than me. He specifically mentioned the story about the *Seahawk*."

As they pulled up to the lighthouse, David slammed on the brakes, sending gravel in all directions. Jim rushed toward the car.

"Follow me," he said, as he led them to the side of the house toward the picket fence above the beach. The dampness from the fog encircled them.

"The police called me early this morning, and I raced over here."

As they reached the edge, they looked down to the beach. Claire gasped and put her hand over her mouth.

"Oh, my God," David said, as he looked down to see a fishing vessel resting with her bow up on the beach and the stern still partly in the water, seemingly reaching out from the thick fog of the sea. The name, although faded, was still readable—SEAHAWK.

"Come on," Jim said. "Let's get down there."

The three of them walked around to the path leading down to the beach. The incline was steep, causing Claire to slip in her attempt to keep up with the men.

"Be careful," Jim said, stopping to help her up.

With Claire back on her feet, the three of them proceeded down the incline. There were large stones on either side of the path, groupings separated by patches of tall sea grass. Their stride was immediately impeded on reaching the sand. A short distance ahead was a group of police officers standing near the craft.

"When did they call you?" David asked.

"About half past five this morning."

The magnitude of the vessel listing to one side had become more apparent as they got closer. The white hull was covered with streaks of rust, all the windows were gone, and the paint was in various stages of corrosion.

Approaching the scene, Jim said, "Sergeant, this is David Parker. He's the guy I was telling you about who's reporting on the *Seahawk*."

David reached out to shake his hand.

"Well, you have one hellava report on your hands, young fella," the sergeant said, as he shook his hand. Got a call early this morning from a woman; said she was taking a walk along the beach and came across this old boat that had run aground. Didn't think much of it, until we got down here and saw it for ourselves. I know Jim here; figured he'd like to see what happened, since she landed right under that lighthouse. That was a pretty good storm we had last night," he went on. "But I didn't think it'd be strong enough to blow a dragger up on shore from forty four years ago," he laughed.

Claire, unable to take her eyes off the vessel, began to walk toward it.

"Ma'am, I suggest you don't go any closer," the sergeant said, leading her back away from the boat.

"Sergeant Collins."

"Mike, about time you showed up."

Taking advantage of the sergeant's distraction, David went to the vessel. He grabbed a railing and pulled himself up onto the deck. He noticed officers were gathered in the wheelhouse.

Claire, who was now determined to find out why

197

the sergeant didn't want her near the boat, quickly walked around the two men and came up behind David. Discovering that Claire was behind him, David turned, took her hand, and pulled her up onto the sloped deck. Together, they approached the wheelhouse where another police officer stopped them. Looking past the officer, they could see what had the men's attention.

"You might not want to see this," the officer said.

There in the wheelhouse was a man with the tattered remnants of clothing still clinging to his bones.

David and Claire stared in disbelief.

"There are more remains below, five men total," the officer said.

***

Many people who gathered for the funeral of Captain Scott Spear and his crew did not know them in life, but these men were part of the town of Stuart Cove and, for that reason, St. Margaret's Church was filled to capacity. David and Claire sat hand-in-hand, as Father Kealy comforted his flock, helping them come to terms with the events that had taken place. Both Helen and Cynthia were in attendance, sharing the front pews with other family members of the crew. Following the service, Claire and David gathered with others in the yard.

"David."

David turned around to see Mary from the Fishhook Pub. "Hi, Mary," he said, as she gave him a friendly hug.

"I understand you decided to move to Stuart Cove."

"Yes, I did."

Mary turned to Claire. "Good job, honey," she said and turned to catch up with a friend, as he passed by.

David and Claire gave each other a look of amusement at this statement. Then, a moment later,

Cynthia approached them. "Cynthia, how are you?" David said, clasping her hands in his.

"My mother would like to talk to you. She's over there," Cynthia said in a soft voice.

"Certainly," he replied.

The three of them walked over to Helen who was sitting in a chair.

"I'm glad to see you, Helen," David said.

"I hear tell Danny's light was on the night before they were found," Helen said.

"Really," David said, trying to appear surprised.

Helen took David by the hand and pulled him down, so she could look into his eyes. "I want to thank you for bringing him home."

David did not know quite what to say, but he realized at that moment that she knew everything.

"It's what Danny wanted," he finally replied.

As they left, Claire asked David, "How did she know?"

"I'm not sure, but she did."

Epilogue

As Camelia Wright turned the bend, three miles out from the Lost and Found Antique Shop in Devon, England, she realized that, in her haste to close early, she had forgotten to take the vintage Caravelle wristwatch she had promised to bring to Mrs. Walker. Knowing that turning back now would further delay her arrival at her sister's birthday party, she hesitated. Darn the luck, *Camelia thought.* Mrs. Walker was so looking forward to receiving that watch. *Her mind made up, she turned around and headed back to the shop.*

The late afternoon sun still offered enough illumination to fill the shop, as Camelia went straight to the back office to retrieve the forgotten watch. There it is, just where I left it, *she thought, reaching out to take the watch from the desktop. Turning to leave, Camelia suddenly froze. As she drew in a strong gasp, her eyes fixed on the body of a young woman lying motionless on the floor.*

Then, a sound, a sound of someone in the shop. Her mind was racing—who is this woman—is she dead—perhaps he didn't see me; *and then, she heard the footsteps coming closer ....*

It had been so quiet in the cramped bedroom/converted office that he jumped when the phone rang.

"David speaking," he said instinctively, as his concentration was suddenly interrupted from his writing.

"Good afternoon, David, I heard you were in town. This is Ellen from Stuart Cove Realty. Do you remember me?"

Claire walked into the study with the cordless phone in her hand. "Sorry to disturb your writing, but it's for you. It's Owen Ladd," she said, as she handed him the phone.

"That's the paranormal investigator from New York," David said, as he took the phone.

"Owen, how the hell are you?"

"Hey, David, I've been trying to reach you. I talked to Emerson, and he told me what happened."

"Sorry about that, Owen. I've been darn busy. A lot going on here. So, what do you think about the *Seahawk*?"

"That's incredible, man. I figured they wanted the light back on, but to tell you the truth, I didn't really know what would happen. That's awesome," Owen said.

"Now, I have to complete my second promise to Danny."

"What's that?"

"I have to tell his story," David said, as he put his arm around Claire's waist.

"You have one hell of a story to tell. So, how are things at the lighthouse—any more experiences?" Owen asked.

"No, it's quiet right now, but that's going to change soon."

"Yeh?" Owen questioned.

"Nothing paranormal. Instead, there's going to be one hell of a party there."

"A party?"

"The place is very special to Claire and me, as you can imagine. So, we got permission to be married there May 19."

"How cool is that? Congratulations."

"Consider yourself invited," David said, kissing Claire's hand.

"I will definitely be there," Owen responded.

David patted down the earth around the lilies, and taking his whiskbroom, he carefully brushed the dirt off the bricks.

"Whatcha doing?" a young boy asked David, as his mother and father read the inscriptions on the fisherman's memorial.

"I'm taking care of this garden for a friend," David said to the boy.

Standing up and brushing the dirt off his pants, David approached the couple. "It doesn't tell the whole story."

They both stared at David, each with a puzzled look on their faces.

"What do you mean by that?" the man asked.

"That memorial, it doesn't tell the whole story," David replied. Gathering his garden utensils, he continued, "If you want the whole story, you'll have to read *The Legend of the Seahawk*."

In Appreciation

I would like to express my gratitude to the United States Lighthouse Society, a non-profit historical and educational organization. Their organization educates and informs those who are interested in lighthouses, both past and present.

If you would like more information about lighthouses or would like to make a donation, please contact:

United States Lighthouse Society
9005 Point No Point Rd. NE
Hansville, WA 98340
ph. 415.362.7255
E-mail: info@uslhs.org
http://www.uslhs.org

4304311

Made in the USA
Charleston, SC
28 December 2009